Once Upon A Silver Strand

An Enchanted Realms Novella

MICHELLE MILES

To the dreamers, the stargazers, and the ones who braid magic into the ordinary, this one's for you.

CHAPTER 1

T he stars whispered louder on the nights she dreamed of cutting her hair. Blinking and twinkling high above in the indigo sky, they watched through the tower window, casting pale silver light across the stone floor. And when the starlight touched her braid, her strands illuminated in that cold, silvery light.

Ariadne had never seen the world beyond her tower window. Never experienced the warm sunlight on her face. Never touched the cool grass under her bare feet. She remained hidden away from the world. Cursed—or blessed—to live her days alone.

She spent long nights gazing at the stars. She had them memorized. How they danced during summer storms and faded to ghost-like shimmers during the winters. How they seemed to give her life and energy as they beamed down into her tower window. And how her strength ebbed when the clouds covered them.

Her initial memories involved that tower, the sky, and her caretaker—an elderly woman whose face, though lined, was kind. She said her hair consisted of moonlight and starlight. Spun from the last breath of a dying star. She said her long hair tethered her to this place—this mortal realm. She said her silver strands had a curse.

That severing her hair would cause her madness. That the sky would rip open, forever altering the realm.

As a child, she believed the stories. Now that she had matured, she remained unsure. But she did not dare tempt fate by cutting her hair. What would happen if she was no longer bound to this place? What would she become? Would she be free to leave, to live a different life, no longer in solitude?

Tonight, the stars were restless. Deep within her, something ancient stirred as though her soul sensed a change. Ariadne couldn't pinpoint the odd impulse deep within her. But she felt restless, like the stars.

She rose from the bed and gazed up at the murals along the tower walls. These recounted her life's journey from birth to when starlight became woven into her hair. To even the moment she was placed in the tower with the woman who was her caretaker. When the woman died, she turned into sparkling, twinkling light and joined the stars above. The enchanted tower continued to provide for her years after her death.

Palpable loneliness, memories of stories long past, and bookshelves containing fantastical tales were all that remained for her.

No end existed.

Would there ever be?

Days and nights blended into one another, marked only by the passing seasons.

Spring brought bright sunshine, a verdant lawn at the base of the tower, and flowers blooming in bright colors she longed to see up close.

The summer proved long, hot, and her least favorite month when days appeared endless and sultry nights seemed eternal.

When autumn arrived, it was as if a deep breath expelled into the world, cooling the air and bringing back the bright, cheerful stars overhead, including her favorite, Andromeda. The wind shifted to the north. The rains came. The foliage changed from bright green to magnificent colors of yellow, orange, red, and gold.

Winter brought the snows. The cold air. The clouds. The dismal darkness. She kept the one window shuttered against the cold and spent days and nights wrapped in cozy blankets with a book. But there were moments she couldn't stop staring at the night sky despite the frigid temperatures.

Now, as summer gave way to the autumn winds, something else shifted. Something had changed.

More than anything, she yearned for freedom from her tower prison. She had never dared to leave, for she feared the consequences.

The caretaker told her, more than once, it was forbidden.

"The world is dangerous, Ariadne. You must stay here. Stay hidden. For there are those who would use you and the starlight in your hair for their own gain."

"What gain? Who?" she had asked.

The caretaker said, "Men with dark hearts. They will cut your hair and use the magic of the stars."

A cryptic response. She never understood what that meant. No matter how many times she asked, the answer remained the same.

Outside her tower, the light shifted suddenly. Odd colors in green, blue, and purple splashed across the stone flooring, catching her attention.

She hurried to the window, where the afternoon breeze turned cool. A metallic twang floated on the air, as though a harbinger of what was to come.

Overhead, clouds gathered. But not any clouds. Not normal clouds. Vibrant, swirling colors suddenly filled the sky. Emerald green. Fiery orange. Electric blue. Colliding. Crashing. Spiraling. Swirling.

Different.

Ariadne had seen enough of the sky beyond her window to understand this was something different. Something dangerous. Something distressing.

An ominous energy flashed through the colorful clouds. As though gathering strength. Lightning sparkled, dancing across the shadows and then shooting downward, disappearing behind the tree line. It appeared to come from the cosmos itself. From behind her earthly bindings far into the heavens. Blinding bursts of energy crackled to life, lifting the hair on the back of her neck.

The clouds shifted. Beyond them, through the break, she saw the shifting of the stars. As though they pushed and pulled against each other. As through warring for dominance. For control. A furious dance on a cosmic grand scale.

She had never seen anything like it.

An overwhelming sense of fear pulsed through her. Yet she couldn't look away as the sky manifested raw, untamed power vibrant with energy.

The unknown swirled above her. A cracking *boom* sounded. A whisper of power slipped through from overhead. The sky splintered in an awesome display of phenomenal cosmic power, surging with a blinding fury.

A bolt of yellow-orange light exploded, illuminating her tiny tower in magnificent light. A loud rumbling followed as she ducked, huddling on the cold stone floor.

Then silence fell.

Still.

Dark.

As though nothing at all happened. But then she smelled the acrid tang of something sharp and metallic. She stood and took a tentative step to the window and peered out. All seemed normal until...

On the charred ground, a figure lay curled in a ball. That figure was a man.

Chapter 2

Ariadne's caretaker left her books. She read them over and over. One about a lost world where starlight held magic and moonlight was powerful. Another told of a romance between a lost princess and a thief who struck a bargain. He took her on a journey to the starlight at the top of the world, and she gave him a strand of her magical hair in return.

She long dreamed of a way to escape her tower prison, but never thought there was a way.

Until today.

Below her, the man curled on the ground could be her way out. She peered over the edge of the window down below. The man had not moved. He lay curled into a ball in the center of the crater, the charred earth surrounding him.

She waited, her breathing shallow, for the man to move. When he didn't, she feared he was dead. She called down.

"Hello?"

No movement. No response.

"Are you all right?" she called again.

He emitted a faint groan, but loud enough for her to hear. He was alive.

He rolled to a sitting position, his knees propped up and a hand on his head. She leaned further out as much as she dared.

"Do you need help?"

The words escaped her before she stopped them. It was a risk to offer help. Her caretaker warned her of strangers. They were dangerous, after all.

He lifted his head and looked up at her. From the distance, it was hard to see much about his features. All she clearly made out was the color of his eyes. A startling blue.

"Are you hurt?" she asked.

He scanned the exterior of the tower. "I'm all right. Is there a way up there?"

He wanted to come up? Fear skipped through her. There had never been anyone else in the tower except for the caretaker. And she was gone for the last several years.

As for a way in, there wasn't. No doors. No windows save for the one she peered out. No way for anyone else to enter.

"No," she said.

He lifted his face to look up at her. "Are you Ariadne?"

Surprise then suspicion flooded her. Her heart skipped. "Yes. Who are you? How do you know my name?"

"Throw down a rope and I'll answer all your questions."

"I have no rope."

She had something better—her hair. But dare she let him in her tower? She didn't know him. She wasn't sure she could trust him. He was a stranger. A stranger who had her name.

The caretaker's words echoed in her mind.

Men with dark hearts. Dangerous men.

"My name is Cassian. I mean you no harm," he called. "I come to beseech you for help." He held up his hands as though in surrender. As though showing he was unarmed would alleviate any fears.

Still, she hesitated. She stepped back from the window into the shadows of her solitude, pressing a hand against her chest to stop the wild thump of fear and unease.

What help could she give this man who fell from the sky? She was no one of importance. What did she have to offer a sky-fallen stranger?

Her hair. Her magical hair was made of starlight and moon shadow. Had he come for that?

"Ariadne, I promise no harm will come to you," he called from below.

What good was his word? The promise of a stranger?

She moved back to the window and glanced down. "How can I trust you? You are a stranger. And strangers are dangerous."

Cassian dropped his hand and paced the area of the charred crater. He paused, his startling eyes returning to her face.

"I understand. But I fell from the stars in the hopes I would find you. And I did."

"Who sent you?"

"No one sent me."

"Then how did you know about me?"

With his face tilted up toward her, he remained mute. At this distance, she was unable to see his expression. He dropped his head, clenched and unclenched his fists as though in indecision. Then he looked back up at her.

"I know about you because of the prophecy."

Cassian watched as the girl stepped away from the open window, disappearing into the shadowy depths of the tower. He waited, the only sound the rustle of the treetops in the faint evening breeze. Twilight was upon them, and soon, it would be full on dark.

Telling her about the prophecy was a risk. But Cassian had taken greater ones.

He had to know if it was true. If she was true.

Calling her by name was a desperate gamble. No more than a half-whispered myth scraped from the corners of forgotten archives.

The stories spoke of a princess hidden from a tyrant who feared her existence. A girl not born of flesh and blood, but of starlight and longing. The final spark of love between two celestial gods torn apart by decree and distance.

Her mother, the Weaver of Dawn. Her father, the Guardian of Night. And their final vow? A single soul spun of both light and shadow.

Ariadne. A living strand of the stars themselves.

A girl born of silence. A girl bound by starlight. Sever the shadow and restore the night.

Those were the words that changed everything.

He remembered the night he first read them. His fingers trembling over the faded ink, the brittle page curled with time. Something ancient had stirred inside him. Wonder. Dread. The terrible weight of knowing.

From that moment, he couldn't sleep. Not when the stars above began vanishing one by one, like dying embers across the sky. Not when silence crept into the celestial halls.

His world was unraveling, and no one else seemed to see it.

So, he searched. Buried himself in scrolls and tomes until his hands were ink-stained and his eyes gritty with exhaustion. And when no one else would act, he did. That was when the rebellion was born. Quiet at first. A question asked in secret, a truth whispered behind guarded eyes.

Until it became treason.

He knew the cost. Knew he'd be stripped of his station, branded a traitor.

Still, he crossed the Gate.

To find her. To save what remained of the stars. To remind the world of what it had forgotten.

Hope.

"Ariadne?" he called.

Nighttime enveloped him. The tower was nothing more than an outline against the inky blackness. Disappointment flared bright and hot deep within him. He had come all this way, risked death, for nothing. He had harnessed the last power of the celestial flame's last ember. Now that was gone. His hope remained with the girl above.

He started to turn away from the tower and find a place to sleep in the trees for the night, when he heard a swish. Spinning around, he saw it. The streak of silver spilled from the open casement like a falling beam of moonlight drifting down through the darkness. It swayed gently in the night air—back and forth, back and forth—until it kissed the ground with impossible grace.

For a breathless moment, he thought it a trick of starlight. A mirage.

But no.

It was her hair.

Braided in a single, thick rope, it shimmered with a light all its own. Not the cold reflection of the moon, but something deeper—alive, pulsing faintly as though it carried the heartbeat of the stars. Each strand caught the air like woven silver thread, ancient and unbroken, as if the night itself had reached down to touch the earth.

Cassian's throat tightened.

It was true.

The daughter of the celestial gods with the silver hair *was alive*.

"Climb up," she called.

Tentatively, he stretched out a hand and wrapped his fingers around the thick braid. Her hair was soft as the fur of a kitten. The way it sparkled in the moonlight was magnificent and breathtaking. He forced himself to climb.

Up and up he went, using his upper body strength to pull him toward the open casement. When he finally made it, he reached a hand out to grab the edge. Once he was able to pull himself into the opening, he released her hair and stumbled inside. He tumbled to the floor, his chest heaving from exertion as he tried to catch his breath.

He was aware of her presence as she stood aside from the window, tugging her lengthy braid back inside.

When he finally got his bearings, he rolled over and sat up. Nighttime shadows lingered in the room of the tower. Her glowing hair was the only light. When he looked up at her, meeting her gaze, his breath halted in his chest.

If he thought her hair was magnificent, her face was incomparable.

Blue eyes sparkled with starlight as she gazed down at him in wonder. Her face was round and delicate, with high cheekbones, a thin nose, and a long neck. A violet gown hugged her slender body, skimming the tops of her ankles. She was barefoot. Everything about her was perfect.

She was, after all, a daughter of the gods.

Awkward silence permeated the air between them as she peered down at him with curious interest. She was not afraid of him, though he suspected he was the first stranger she'd seen in her life.

"Ariadne." He said her name in reverence. He climbed to his feet and realized he was a head taller than her.

"How do you know my name?" she asked. There was no suspicion in her tone.

"I'm afraid that's a long story." He glanced around the small tower room and spied a chair on the other side. He motioned to it. "May I sit?"

She nodded, though remained where she was. Wary. Cautious. Watching.

He pulled the chair over and lowered down onto the cushion with a sigh. Fatigue pounded through him. Falling through the Celestial Gate was not easy, nor was climbing up to her tower. He rested his hands on his thighs as he tried to regulate his breathing.

"I like stories," she said finally. She dropped to the floor, crossing her legs in front of her with her hands in her lap, and waited.

He smiled. She was innocent and sweet. A quick scan of the room showed a bookshelf full of books, which pleased him. It meant the caretaker who brought her made sure she was well read and educated. Perhaps what he came to tell her would not be that great of a shock to her.

She tipped her head to one side, regarding him. "You fell from the sky. How are you still alive?"

It was a good question.

He smiled—wry, thoughtful. For weeks, he'd prepared for the crossing. There was only once chance to breach the Celestial Gate. One wrong calculation, one hesitation, and he wouldn't have fallen into her mortal realm at all. He would have been reduced to stardust. Or burned alive in the ether between worlds.

His mind worked quietly, choosing his words. How did he explain it?

How did he tell her he was a guardian of Starna, the realm forged of light and shadow—the place between stars? That he had been appointed by the gods themselves to keep the Celestial Gate sealed, its power dormant, its path untrodden?

And then...he found the prophecy. Or, rather, the prophecy came to him. Unbidden. Revealing the truth and her name to him and him alone.

The Starborn Child.

Her.

He had sworn to protect it, to protect her, even if she never knew it.

But the stars changed. The gate trembled. And the realm cracked.

And everything he'd once been meant nothing anymore.

Between light and shadow—dawn and night—she was the key to saving the realm. The realm in which she truly belonged. Not hidden here in the mortal world.

She waited, her eyes sparkling with their starry light and her hands clasped in her lap. How did he tell her?

He took a deep breath, expelled it.

"I'm a guardian from the realm of Starna. And I've come to take you home."

CHAPTER 3

Ariadne stared at him, the shadows concealing his features. With the moonless night, her hair was the only source of light to see anything about him. When he said he had come to take her home, she stiffened, and her mouth had gone dry.

Home? She knew no other home. *This* was her home. This tower. This place hidden away from mortal prying eyes. Keeping her safe. Keeping her secret. Keeping her tethered here.

It was her fate.

She had always known it was her fate.

Even the caretaker told her she would spend her days here, alone, in this tower.

Where it was *safe*.

"Are you...did you hear me?" he asked.

His voice was deep, soft, pleasant. Years passed without her speaking to anyone. At first, she thought his arrival was a welcome one. Though she did not trust him, though she feared him, she allowed him to climb into the tower and sit across from her.

Why?

Her loneliness was an ever-present companion that threatened to consume her. In her chest, a hollow feeling lingered until Cassian arrived.

"I heard you." Her voice was barely above a whisper.

"You don't believe me."

He shifted in the chair, a slight movement, and stretched out one leg. He wore boots with buttons. His pants were tucked neatly into the tops.

"How can I?"

Her gaze drifted back up to his shadowed face.

When he landed inside the window, she got a glimpse of him. He had dark hair. Long enough that it brushed his collar. Beyond that, she knew nothing else.

"I understand. This is all..." He waved his hand to encompass the area.

"Too much," she whispered.

She clenched her hands together, her mind racing with thoughts of how to protect herself. There were no weapons in the tower. But her gaze drifted to the cold hearth, where a fire burned in the coldest depths of winter. There was poker. If she needed to use that, she would.

"Yes, too much," he agreed. "What did your caretaker tell you?"

Her gaze flickered back to him, though in the dark it was difficult to see his expression. "How do you know about my caretaker?"

He remained still, not moving. Except for one hand. His fingers twitched as though he realized he should not have asked that.

"I know many things," he said finally. Then abruptly changed the subject. "Do you have water?"

The kitchen was small but functional. She never wanted for food or drink. It was all simply provided for her. She never questioned it.

"I'll get it for you."

She unfolded her legs and rose, stepping to the small kitchen where she opened an overhead cupboard and pulled out a wooden cup. She removed the lid to the barrel and ladled water into the cup. Returning, she closed the gap between them. When she got closer, he lifted his gaze to meet hers, and it was then that she saw his features for the first time.

Though his blue eyes were dark orbs in the shadows, she saw his square, strong jaw with the dimple in the center. A piece of hair flopped across his forehead, curling at the ends. Eyebrows, straight and narrow, slashed over his eyes. When she approached, he reached up and took the cup from her. Their hands brushed in a brief touch. It sent unexpected tingles through her.

Then he drank it all in one gulp.

"Thank you," he said.

She moved back to her side of the room, leaning against the bookcase with her hands clasped in front of her, eyeing the hearth and the fire poker. Still, she had questions that needed answering.

"How did you come to be here?" she asked. "Before you arrived, there was a storm in the sky. I've never seen anything like it before."

"What sort of storm?" He held the wooden cup, balancing it on his knee.

"The stars seemed to clash. Pulling and pushing against each other. A brilliant light flashed. That's when you appeared."

"The Celestial Gate," he muttered.

She did not understand what that meant.

He lifted his gaze to hers. "What did the caretaker tell you?"

"That it was forbidden for me to leave. That there were men who would cut my hair and use the magic of the stars for their own gain."

Though how they would use the magic of the stars with her hair was not clear to her.

She paused a moment, taking a deep breath. "Are you one of those men? Will you cut my hair?"

"No," he said quickly. "I told you before. I mean you no harm, and I meant it. The caretaker was right, though. Men seek to profit from your hair. Your hair..." He paused, his gaze lingering on the length of the braid as it fell to the floor in a puddle around her. "Your hair is full of stars and moonlight."

"That's what the caretaker told me, too."

"Did this caretaker also tell you about the tower?"

She lifted a brow, intrigued. "What about the tower?"

"It was built for you. To shield you. To hide you. To keep you safe. Until the day came for you to return home and embrace your destiny," he said.

"My home is here," she insisted.

"Your home is not here," he replied.

She folded her arms across her chest. "And where, then, is my home?"

"Your home is the realm of Starna. Through the Celestial Gate. That's where I came from. And that's where I intend to take you."

Hot pinpricks danced along her spine. She did not want to leave here. *This* was her home. She'd spent her entire life here. Most of it alone.

Determination edged through her. She wasn't going with him. "I'm not leaving. It is forbidden."

"No," he said. "No longer. You must come with me, Ariadne. Starna needs you."

She clutched her elbows as fatigue pounded through her. "I will not go. Now, I must sleep, and you must leave."

Without waiting for his reply, she moved to the open casement and tossed out her long braid. When she turned toward him, she waited, her hands clenched at her sides. He unfolded his tall frame from the chair. As he stepped closer to her, she made out more of his features. His expression was stern, determined.

"I'll go for now, but I'm not leaving this realm without you."

He took her hair in his hands and descended from the tower. When he was safely on the ground, she pulled in her hair and gathered it into her arms. A curtained alcove, located across the tower, housed her bed. She slipped inside, closing the curtains behind her and sat on the edge of the bed, thinking of Cassian.

He fell from the sky. He claimed to be from a mysterious realm named Starna. A foreign land he claimed was her home. Why had the caretaker never told her of this?

She shoved those thoughts out of her mind as she pulled her legs up onto the bed, her long braid dusting the floor. She curled into a ball on her side, squeezing her eyes shut, determined to sleep. But his words continued to haunt her.

Cassian trudged into the forest and plopped down on the hard, cold ground. He positioned himself to keep the tower within view. Not that he expected her to escape. It was more of a way for him to keep an eye on the window.

He had made it through the Celestial Gate, certainly, but he wasn't so sure his getaway went unnoticed. He failed to mention to Ariadne several royal guards were on his trail. Not because he intended to plunge through the gate, but because he'd broken out of the dungeon. He was arrested for high treason with his betrayal to the crown and was scheduled for execution in the most horrific way.

He, the Guardian of Knowledge, was an outlaw.

His arrival through the gate not only put his life in jeopardy, but hers. It would only be a matter of time before the usurper's men followed and found them.

Even so, dare he show his face back in Starna? He had no choice, really, as the realm depended upon his return with the girl with starlight hair. He had his work cut out for him, though, as she didn't believe him and refused to leave the mortal realm. Here, she would do nothing but waste away until she was nothing more than stardust. But in Starna...she would be so powerful. The tyrannical king would fear her. The royal court would bow to her. The nobility, the gentry, the peasants would rejoice at her return. Though she was born of divine love, Ariadne was more than a celestial child. She was the rightful heir to the throne of Starna. The one promised by prophecy, chosen by the stars, and forged to reclaim a realm undone by its own power.

He inhaled the sweet scent of the lush greenery around him. Sleep eluded him despite his fatigue. Time was of the essence, and he needed to convince her to come back with him through the gate.

Even now, the realm began to fracture under the iron fist of the present regime. The king stole the throne beneath a broken sky. But she was born to stitch the stars back together when the time was right.

Cassian leaned his back against a tree and pulled his knees to his chest. But as the night dragged on, his fatigue was too much. His eyes drooped and before long, he slept.

CHAPTER 4

S leep eluded her. She laid in her bed staring at the dark ceiling wondering why she cast him out. Guilt washed through her. She should have let him stay and offer him some comfort rather that tossing him to the forest floor.

But the things Cassian said scared her. She had never thought of leaving her tower. Why should she? She had all the necessary comforts she needed. Food, water, clothes, bed, a roof over her head when the seasons changed. She had books—

Books.

She pulled herself out of bed and padded across the stone floor, her bare feet silent as she made her way to the bookshelf. She fumbled in the dark until she found the candleholder and struck a match, lighting it. The warm glow of the candle encircled her as she held it up, looking at the aged spines of the books.

She reached out, placing her fingertip on the leather-bound books, their letters glittering in the candlelight.

Of Gates and Guardians

Celestial Hymns

Lovers who Lit the Sky

Stars and Silence

When she was little, the caretaker read to her. As she grew and learned to read, she read them over and over. She pulled out the thin volume, *Celestial Hymns*, then dropped to her knees. She placed the candleholder aside and flipped open the book. It was written in the common tongue, for the most part, but there were passages in a language she was unable to read. The caretaker never taught her to read it, either. She left that on the floor and stood, picking up another volume. This one was *Of Gates and Guardians*.

The pages were thick, stiff, and smelled musty. This book told of the High Guardians who vowed to protect each of the nine Celestial Gates, one for each of the nine gods. She dropped to the floor once again and read about each one.

The Gate of Dawn, guarded by the Weaver of Dawn. *Can only be opened during the first light of day.*

The Gate of Night, guarded by the Guardian of the Night. *Where all dangerous magic was sealed away.*

The Gate of Storms, guarded by the Bearer of Storms. *Creates power between the celestial realm and the mortal realm.*

Each page was accompanied by a drawing. She paused on the Gate of Storms, her finger tracing the lightning bolt. A spiral of flickering light fractured the sky.

A spiral that reminded her of the one she saw before Cassian landed at the foot of her tower.

Did he come through the Gate of Storms?

Her gaze drifted back down the page as she read.

The Gate of Storms can only be opened by the Bearer of Storms. Then one shall ride through the night with a lightning bolt in one hand, to travel through to the mortal realm. A dangerous practice and forbidden.

But he had come through the gate. And he was here. Alive. Come to take her home, he said. She tossed aside the book and stood, picking another one. A sense of restlessness passed through her as she flipped pages.

She read poetic tales of celestial beings written in fragmented verse that was difficult to understand. *Born of blood under a ruined sky.*

She read an old scholar's account of a vanished kingdom and their guardians that seemed to be nothing more than a bedtime story. But perhaps it was more. *Bound by an unbreakable oath, a binding pact to mend a fractured world.*

She read an allegory about a girl born of starlight who brings rebirth to a realm—or perhaps ruin, depending upon who penned the story. *Burning starlight so bright pierced the shadows.*

She read a lavish history about a celestial monarchy destroyed by war, causing its annihilation. *And he came from the depths of the darkness to conquer, to destroy, to rule.*

There was more. So much more. As she read, she realized these were not mere *stories*. They were something more. Something tangible. Something *real*. Truth. History.

Someone left these books here for her to read, to learn, to understand.

These books were of a place she had never seen and didn't know. A place that belonged somewhere in the stars. A place that was, perhaps, her true home.

Ariadne lifted her head and gazed up at the open casement as the first rays of morning splinted through the clouds.

Dawn.

Putting aside the book in her hand, she rose and padded to the window to look out. Cassian wasn't there. Was he gone?

Turning back into the room, she reached for her candle with the remaining flickering light. It had burned down to a nub. She blew it out and searched for another one.

"Ariadne?"

His voice. Calling her from below. Her heart skipped and climbed its way to her throat. Momentarily frozen, she peered at the open casement.

"Ariadne, let down your hair!" he called again.

Uncertainty flooded her. Her gaze slid to the discarded pile of books on the floor in a semi-circle. Her hands shook. If she allowed him back into the tower, what then? Would he want to take her away to this place he called Starna?

A part of her pounded with the excitement of the unknown, the chance to leave this safe haven and explore a wider world. The other part of her wanted to shrink back into the shadows and hide herself away until her last breath.

But that wasn't living, was it?

What would the caretaker want?

She thought of the aged woman who raised her, kept her safe, loved her. The woman who wanted nothing more than to make sure no one came to cut her hair and destroy her magic, her soul.

But what if...?

What if Cassian was right? What if there *was* a realm behind this one?

She looked at the books again. Her heart pounded so hard and fast it made her gut twist into a knot.

"Ariadne?" A tentative call this time.

On impulse, she darted for the window. She flung her hair out of the opening, letting it fall to the ground below. And then he climbed.

Though he tugged on her hair, it was with an unexpected gentleness. When he arrived, he stepped into the tower. His assessing gaze went over the room, pausing on the pile of books she'd left open and read on the floor. Then his questioning glance came back to her.

Her heart still pounded. She clenched her fists to keep her hands from shaking. Taking a deep breath through her nose, she expelled it through her mouth.

"Is it true?" Her voice shook as she spoke.

He cut a glance at the pile of books again. "Is what true?"

"The realm of Starna. It's real, isn't it?"

Again, he met her gaze. His, unwavering. Strong. Full of life. "It is."

She turned away and headed to the small kitchen area in need of something to do. She busied herself with making tea and putting together a meager breakfast of scones, fruit, and cheese.

Behind her, his feet shuffled across the floor. A glance over her shoulder and she saw he kneeled at the pile of books, picking up one. He scanned a page, turned it, then read another. She turned her attention back to the task at hand, filling the teapot with boiling water, gathering cups and plates and food. She picked up the tray and turned back. Taking a deep breath, she walked to him, placing the tray on the floor near the books, and sat.

"Tea?"

Amusement flickered in his eyes as he nodded. As though he were unsure of her actions. Likely, he wondered if she was trying to remain calm. She was. She did not want to show him how terrified she was of an uncertain future.

Before he arrived, her life was the same. One day blending into the next. The nights were long and lonely. The days equally so.

Nothing different happened. Until yesterday when he arrived on the heels of a magnificent celestial storm.

She poured tea for the both of them and handed him a cup. He took it, sipped, and eyed the food on the tray.

"Help yourself," she said.

She crossed her legs in front of her and held the cup, watching him with uncertainty as he picked fruit and placed it on a plate.

"You've been reading, I see." A nod toward the books on the floor.

"Books the caretaker used to read me. Books about—" She stopped herself, pressed her lips together. She sucked in a breath. "I thought they were fiction, but now..."

"You're unsure?"

"I read about the nine gates guarded by the nine gods."

He froze. Didn't move. Didn't blink as he peered at her. "You have questions."

"I have many questions. I do not know where to start."

She kept her gaze fixed on his long, slender fingers instead of his face. She didn't want to look him in the eye and see the undeniable truth there.

He put down the cup. "I've handled this poorly. You're frightened, I can see. And you have every right to be."

A fluttering of nerves erupted in the pit of her stomach as she forced herself to meet his gaze. "Did you come through the Gate of Storms?"

Indecision flashed through his eyes. His lips thinned as though he did not want to answer. Finally, he nodded. "I did."

Ariadne put down the cup, her appetite gone and her mouth dry. "Who are you?"

He swallowed hard, his throat working. "I am the Guardian of Knowledge. Appointed by the Goddess of Echoes."

"The Goddess of Echoes." She whispered the words in reverence as the memory of the text resurfaced. She was the keeper of the Gate of Echoes, where all divine knowledge was stored. Past, present, and future. What once was. What would come to be.

He nodded. "She chose me to guard the ancient Temple of Silence, where all knowledge resides."

The Temple of Silence was a place of reverence. A place where only those appointed were allowed to step foot inside. At least, according to the text she read.

"Why? Why were you chosen?" she asked.

"She said I had the courage to carry the truth."

"What truth?" The question burned through her, though she was terrified of the answer.

"The truth of you. She told me I would remember what others forgot, that I would discover the name of the girl. It is a burden I've carried for many years. When the usurper conquered the realm, he twisted ancient prophesies, told lies to the people, and cut off access to true knowledge. He erased our history, our world as we knew it, and replaced it with these fabrications. Lies. Deceit. He destroyed all that the realm of Starna was. Dismantling it piece by piece. I watched it fall under his dark rule."

Telling her this weighed heavily on him. Sorrow and fear, desperation and need lined his face. As though he were stripped bare and laid his emotions at her feet. She struggled to imagine such a world since the one she lived in for all of her twenty years was full of silence and stars, spinning seasons, and solitude. No one ruled her.

"Why did he do this?" she asked.

"For power. For control. For his own personal gain. He declared the age of peace to be over, and he chose himself as the one to rule the stars and the gods. The heir to the throne was long rumored to be dead. The heir is not dead." His eyes glittered with hope as he peered at her.

Her chest constricted. When she spoke, her voice was a roughened whisper. "Who is the heir?"

"This will not be easy for you to hear," he said. "Long ago, the gods swore a blood oath. If Starna should fall, its true heir would be born not of a crown, but of sacrifice. The gods themselves chose the heir, by the stars, forged to reclaim a realm undone by the usurper.

"As the sky fractured, and the constellations vanished, the gods moved but not quickly enough to stop the collapse. The heir was born in secret and hidden away by the last loyal guardians of the gods. Raised and protected by a caretaker until it was time for the heir's return."

Suddenly lightheaded, Ariadne pressed a hand against her forehead.

"*He stole the throne beneath a broken sky. She was born to stitch the stars back together. Where starlight falls, the heir shall rise. And the shadow throne shall crumble beneath her name.*" He scooted closer to her, reaching for her hand. His fingers curled around hers. "You, Ariadne. You are the heir."

CHAPTER 5

T he *heir.*

Ariadne stared at Cassian from her prone position, her heart drumming her chest. How was this possible? Part of her wanted to reject it. She was *not* the heir. This was all a cruel joke or, worse, a dream. When she woke, she'd still be alone in the silent tower with only the sounds of stars twinkling overhead to comfort her.

Getting his words out of her mind was hard. Everything he told her rang true to the words she'd read in the books. Now she understood how all the pieces fit together. The caretaker left the books for her so she'd know, she'd understand. But not once did the caretaker tell her of her true lineage.alce

The gods swore a blood oath.

The true heir was born of sacrifice.

"Say something. Please," he whispered in the faint morning light.

"I do not know what to say."

She pressed cold fingertips to her lips and looked at the open casement. Searching. But for what, she didn't know.

Cassian sipped his tea, made a face, and set it aside. No doubt it had grown cold as he spoke. She remained rooted in place. When once she knew exactly who she was, now she was uncertain. Her life forever altered by the arrival of the man sitting across from her.

The part of her wanting to reject his words dwindled away to nothing. There was no malice in his face. No dishonesty. Nothing to indicate what he told her was a falsehood.

"I want to believe you," she said.

"But?"

"But I am afraid." It hurt to admit it to him.

"I know." Guilt lined his face. "I didn't want to be the one to tell you." He fiddled with a grape between his thumb and forefinger. Something troubled him. As though there were more truths he had yet to share with her.

"The caretaker told me men wanted my hair. To use for their own power. That is true, isn't it?"

"Yes," he said, softly. Morning light slashed across his booted feet from the open window. He turned his face toward it, his blue eyes fixed on the outside world. He took a deep breath, expelled it. "There is more I need to tell you."

When he didn't speak again for a long moment, she rose from the floor and stepped to him. She dropped to her knees in front of him, taking his hands in hers. It was a gesture of trust.

"Please tell me everything, Cassian."

He looked down at her, his eyes meeting hers. The light of curiosity danced in his gaze. And for a moment, she felt as though she saw right to the depths of his soul. She understood him. She understood he had to be the one to come to her, to tell her the truth, to spirit her away back to the mystical realm of Starna. A place she had never heard of until his arrival.

"It will be difficult to return to Starna," he said.

"Through the Gate of Storms?"

He shook his head. "We cannot return that way. It is sealed on the other side."

"Then how?"

He pressed his lips together and looked away, as though he had the answer but wasn't ready to share it with her.

"In the Temple of Silence, I found the old tomes and scrolls about what the gods did. How they intended to save the realm should it fall." He glanced back down at her. "I found you."

Something about the way he said it sent a shudder through her.

"I knew it was forbidden. I knew the usurper didn't want this information found. He tried to destroy the Temple of Silence. He could not. It is protected by divine power. Only the gods can destroy that which they made."

A strange sensation skipped up her spine as his face turned grave.

"When I found you, I went to the High Guardian to tell him in the hopes he would find a way to save the realm. Instead, he betrayed me."

She sucked in a breath.

"I was arrested for high treason and thrown into the royal dungeons awaiting execution."

"Oh," she breathed. "You escaped?"

He nodded. "With help. There are those who wish to see Starna restored to its former glory. They helped me escape through the Gate of Storms. The leader...he..."

He clamped his mouth shut as he looked away, back to the open window, as though that would give him the courage he needed to continue. She squeezed his hands in encouragement.

"He was my friend, and he gave his life for my escape."

Sorrow flooded her. The anguish on his face made her gut twist. "I'm so sorry."

He dropped to the floor in front of her, clasping her hands in his and holding them against his chest. "Don't be. It was worth it to make it here to you. Ariadne, don't let his death be for nothing. Come back with me to Starna. Fight with us. Reclaim your throne and your world."

His impassioned plea was like a knife to her heart. How was she to leave this place, this sanctuary? How was she supposed to become this mystical person born of the gods blood oath?

She pulled her hands free and rose, stepping back from him. Indecision speared her. Weighed on her. She was not the hero he wanted her to be. She was not ruler material. She was nothing but a girl living alone in a tower. Waiting for...

What?

Her life to be over?

Or her life to begin?

Was Cassian's arrival the harbinger of new beginnings?

His upturned face held hope.

"Cassian, I...I cannot."

His shoulders drooped as he got to his feet. Disappointment creased his face as he turned away, back to the window. He leaned on the open casement, unable to look at her.

"I understand. I hope you know I had to try."

The sea of guilt was vast, nearly consuming her. She said nothing as she picked up the dishes and the tray of food from the floor. On silent feet, she carried it to the small kitchen and dropped it on the counter. She leaned there, the weight of knowledge bearing down on her.

She stared down at the half-eaten meal looking for answers. There were no answers there.

Indecision flared through her, bright and hot, as she turned from the counter to look at him.

He stood at the window, his back muscles taut and tension emanating off him. He peered out into the morning. Though she was unable to see his face, she knew there was disappointment there. Regret. Grief.

He'd risked it all to come here. To find her.

She turned him away. Refused him.

Her feet moved before she realized her mind had made up to do it. And then she was standing next to him at the window. He turned his head, looking down at her with question burning in his gaze.

"I'm just an ordinary girl," she whispered.

"No, you're not. You're extraordinary. I wish you knew how extraordinary you are."

Heat flooded her as she moved to stand closer to him. He smelled of petrichor and something sharp and pungent—the scent of the stars or perhaps lightning.

She slipped her hand into his. "If I go with you, will you be there? With me?"

His face remained impassive. "Every step of the way. Until you sit on the throne. I give you my solemn vow. From this day until that one."

Ariadne glanced away to the cool autumn morning greeting the land. She took a deep breath, expelled it, and made her decision.

"Then I will go. I will return with you to Starna. And I will reclaim my birthright."

Saying the words out loud sent a quivering of fear through her.

His hand tightened on hers. If he was happy with her answer, he didn't show it.

"But," she added, "I don't know the way."

"We cannot go back through the Gate of Storms."

He released her and ran his hand down the length of her braid hanging down her back, spilling onto the floor in a puddle of moonlight and starlight behind her.

"But there is a way." His voice was soft in her ear, as though he spoke a secret.

"How?"

His fingers wrapped around her braid, drawing it forward with quiet purpose. The weight of it settled across his palm—thick, silvery, still warm from where it had rested against her back. The strands shimmered like captured moonlight against his sun-golden skin.

He stared at it like it wasn't hair at all.

Like it was a map. A key. A solution.

She could feel it—his intention—not violent, but sharp with need. A strand or two. That's all he thought it would take. Just enough to tear open a way back to where he'd come.

Back to Starna.

His gaze lingered on the weave, reverent but restless. Like he was on the edge of something holy and dangerous, and all he had to do was sever the thread.

Ariadne's gut clenched.

She stepped back, heart pounding, the braid slipping from his hand. Her head shook before words could catch up. She didn't know what would happen if he cut it. Neither did he.

But something deep in her bones whispered, *Once it starts, it doesn't stop.*

"No," she said.

"We must. One strand. Maybe two—"

"No," she said again, this time her voice was firmer.

But there was something that told her he *knew* this was the answer, though he hadn't shared it. He knew this was the way back to the starlight realm, back to his world. Had she dug deep enough in the books, in the lore, would she have found it? Would she, too, have the answer?

He dropped his hand to his side. "You're right, of course. It is something I should not ask."

He didn't understand the caretaker told her over and over of the consequences of cutting her hair. She'd face madness. An unraveling of her soul. Destruction from the inside out.

"The caretaker...she...she told me—"

"I will never use it to hurt you or others." His eyes flashed fire as he said it. "*Never.* You must know that."

"I don't know *you*," she pointed out.

His jaw clenched, the muscles flexing along the edge. "No, you don't. You have no reason to trust me or believe what I've told you. The caretaker was right—there are men who will come to take your hair, to use you to gain more power to control the realm of all eternity. Ariadne, I—"

Thunder rumbled in the distant sky. They both snapped their attention to the open window, still flooded with morning light. There were no clouds in sight. No indication of a thunderstorm and yet the sky rumbled.

Cassian leaned against the casement, his face upturned to the sky as he peered out. His hands tightened on the ledge, his back stiff and taut as a bowstring.

"The gates," he whispered.

She rushed to his side. The sky should have been brilliant blue. Cloudless. But instead, the morning sun dimmed as though it passed behind a shadow. A sudden shift in the air from the autumn breeze to something sharp and metallic, crackling with the thunderous boom that rolled across the expanse of sky.

The sun was gone in an instant replaced by the glittering stars overhead in an indigo sky. How could this be?

She watched in fascination as the stars—the ones she'd memorized from the time she was a child—shifted. Warped. Changed.

Cassian jerked back from the window, stumbling over her braid that was coiled around the floor.

"He found me. Get away from the window, Ariadne." His voice was stern, sharp.

"What is it?"

The moment the words were out of her mouth, it happened.

The stars fell.

Streaks of bright white light smeared across the sky in a brilliant display of cosmic power. She sucked in a breath as she watched, mystified and horrified.

"Get away from the window!" he shouted.

But she did not obey.

She was enthralled.

Birds scattered. Forest animals scurried away. Shadows appeared where there should have been none. Overhead, the clouds spiraled out of control. Churning. Twisting. Spinning. Creating the strangest vortex she had ever seen with veins of gold and violet light streaking through it. Colors that did not belong to the dawn. Colors she had never seen before.

The wind whipped into a frenzy. A thrumming took up residence deep within her as she watched the sky crack and bleed with the magnificent colors. As though space folded in on itself right above her tower.

And then the gate tore open in a blinding, brilliant burst of starlight.

"Ariadne!"

His sharp tone spurred her into action. She spun from the window and took a step, tripping over her hair. She pitched forward, but he caught her in his arms, holding her steady. She cowered against him, shivering with the terror shifting through her.

"The gate—" she started.

"I know," he said. "Somehow, the usurper opened it. They are coming. We have to leave this place."

His gaze flickered around the small tower looking for an escape. There was none.

"There is no way out." She reached for her thick braid, pulling a portion over her shoulder. "What will happen if I cut it?"

He shook his head. "I only know what I read in the scrolls in the Temple."

A thunderous boom sounded on the ground outside the tower. The earth vibrated. The tower walls shuddered.

She spun away from him, panic tightening her chest, her eyes scanning for something sharp. But before she could take a step toward the kitchen, Cassian reached for the dagger at his hip and held it out to her.

She didn't hesitate. She grabbed it and pressed it back into his hands.

"We have to try," she said, breathless.

He looked at her, uncertainty flickering in his eyes. "Are you sure?"

Below them, voices rose even closer now. A sudden clang rang out as a grappling hook latched onto the windowsill, rope snapping taut. They were coming. For her.

"We have to try," she repeated, louder this time.

Her hands moved to her temple, fingers diving into the braid that had never once been cut, not in all her life. She tugged free a thick lock and held it out to him.

Cassian swallowed hard, then raised the blade.

The dagger slid through the strands with a clean, sharp whisper. And just like that, a piece of hair was cut. The air around them sparked with starlight.

She waited, holding her breath. They both did. And for a long, agonizing moment, nothing happened.

He took the sliced strand between his fingers and placed the knife close to her head. In that instant, their eyes met. His full of apology and torment as he hesitated.

"Do it," she whispered before she lost the courage.

The blade touched her hair, making the strands shimmer and glow. When he sliced through, he held the piece in his hand. They both watched in wonder as the strands broke apart and dissolved into tiny motes of silver light shaped like stars. The stream floated upward, weightless, like sparkles released from glowing embers. They swirled around each other. Dancing. Twirling. Gyrating. Until they merged as one.

Then, a burst of light and a swirling vortex appeared in front of them. Without waiting another moment, he replaced his dagger, grabbed her hand and dove inside, pulling her along with him.

CHAPTER 6

His hand was tight on hers as they tumbled through the swirling light. She fell into the back of him trying to keep her footing but it was almost impossible as they tumbled through space. Then the vortex spit them out as though something foul. She collided with him as they tumbled to the ground and rolled several feet. She halted next to him, her head throbbing and her heart beating a wild beat.

She'd done it. She'd cut it. Just one strand, barely the width of her pinky. But still, it was her hair. Her magic. Her lifeline.

She held her breath, waiting.

The strand had turned to starlight the moment it left his fingers, unraveling into the wind like silver smoke to open the portal. Now the air around her stilled, as if the entire realm of Starna listened, watching, waiting.

Hoping.

Her heart pounded.

One. Two. Three.

Nothing shattered. No madness clawed up from her chest. Her soul didn't implode. The sky didn't rip itself open to swallow her whole.

The caretaker had lied.

Instead, a hush fell over the land. Not silence. Reverence. Like the realm recognized the offering for what it was. A signal. A promise. A return.

Hope.

The braid on her back warmed. Not burning but awakening. She hadn't been punished. She'd been noticed.

She stared up at the strangest sky she'd ever seen. It flickered. Not with stars or moonlight but something else, something that did not make sense. Her brows drew together as she peered upward at the night.

Swirling clouds shrouded the sky blocking out the stars. Dark menacing clouds that seemed to control all there was and all there would ever be. As she scanned the world overhead, she realized it was *not* clouds—but the absence of stars.

Near her, Cassian crawled toward her on his belly, suddenly at her side. A hand slid around her waist as he anchored himself to her. Bright blue eyes full of question and concern met hers.

"Are you hurt? Can you move?"

Before she answered, he sucked in a breath and bolted upright. Pale light reflected in his face. Confusion etched through her.

"Ariadne...your...hair." His words were broken, soft, full of wonder.

She saw it then. The braid trailing behind and around her on the cool ground. It glowed. Shimmered. Pulsed. Shined with an inner light. All the way down to the tip of her braid. She sat up suddenly, her head objecting to the quick movement. A throbbing pounded her temples.

He scooted closer to her, reaching for her hair to run a hand down the length.

"By all the gods and saints," he whispered. "It's incredible."

He reached for her hand, taking it in his, and placing it on the thick plait. She felt it then. A pulsing sensation through the strands. As though they were alive with their own magic.

"What's it doing?" Panic laced her tone.

"You're a child of Starna. Perhaps it recognizes you."

Shouts rose. His head snapped toward it. She realized then they were in a meadow. Tall grasses waved in the evening breeze. The thunder of hooves pounded the ground, vibrating it beneath her.

"We have to go." He held a hand down to her.

She didn't think, didn't hesitate as she grabbed it. He hauled her to her feet. They took off at a run through the meadow, her bare feet in the cool grass. She didn't have time to take in the wonderful sensation as they ran. She wanted to spend a lifetime exploring the trees and the world now that she had escaped her tower.

The thought hit her like a punch in the gut, and she came to a shuddering halt.

She had escaped her tower.

It took a moment for Cassian to realize she'd stopped. He halted, turned back to her. In the shadowy darkness, his face was pinched with worry, concern, and a hint of fear.

"What is it? What's wrong?" he demanded, his tone urgent.

More shouts in the distance. Behind her, she saw the men on horseback riding toward them. Torches held aloft to light their way. The only light surrounding them was that of her hair glowing and pulsing like a guiding beacon in the night. But now she was paralyzed with indecision and fright. What had she done?

"I'm here," she said.

But what she meant to say was *she was here in Starna.* This mythical realm she had never heard of until Cassian crashed into her life. He hurried toward her, reaching for her. His hands landed on her upper arms while his eyes watched the approaching men on horseback.

"Yes, you're here. With me. We have to go, Ariadne." Then his gaze flickered over the length of her hair. "And somehow hide your hair. It's leading them right to us."

Panic swelled inside her. "Cassian, I can't do this. I thought I could but I...can't."

He pulled her close to him, his hands gently rubbing up and down her arms. "You can."

She shook her head. "No. I'm not strong enough. I—"

"You are."

Then he wrapped his arms around her in a tight embrace. He held her, his chin resting on top of her head in a moment of calm. As if they had all the time in the world. She was so stunned by the physical contact, she wasn't sure how to react. But then the warmth of his body seeped into her and that loamy scent of him lingered on his skin. Her body went limp against his and all she wanted for the rest of her life was Cassian holding her. Like this. Forever.

"I believe in you," he whispered. Then he pulled back, holding her at arm's length. "Look what you did already."

"I didn't."

"*You did*. Your hair did. Your hair brought us here, back to Starna. Because you belong here."

The men on horseback were getting closer. He took her hand.

"I will protect you. I will keep you safe. I swear this as my solemn vow to you."

Her heart climbed to her throat. She gave a quick nod, and they took off again through the tall meadow grass heading toward the edge of the trees in front of them. They were dark, standing like silent sentries in the dead of night. The moment they stepped beneath the canopy, the air shifted, growing thick. Wet and heavy. Clinging to her like a damp cloth. Breathing was more difficult. The scent of rain and earth permeated the air, filling her lungs. Sounds dulled. Even the birds were silent. Like stepping into something ancient. Older than time itself.

The forest floor was unkind to her bare feet. She cried out as she stepped on something sharp and jerked her hand free of his, halting. She pitched forward, her hands on her knees as she tried to catch her breath.

"Wait, please."

"You're barefoot. I forgot," he said. He was at her side in an instant, his hand on her back. "I'll find you some shoes. Are you all right?"

"I stepped on something sharp." Though she wanted to be brave, a whimper escaped her.

Without a word, he swept her into his arms as though she weighed nothing. He cradled her against the solid warmth of his chest as he stepped through the bracken. Her heart tripped. She forgot how to breathe.

"This isn't necessary," she objected, weakly.

"Shh. It is. I'll find someplace safe for us to hide and then we will deal with the rest."

"What about the men on horseback?" she asked.

"They won't follow us in here. The forest is too dense for them on horseback."

"They could follow on foot," she said.

He gave her a thin-lipped response, as though he hadn't through of that.

A grin wanted to erupt, but she managed to suppress it. Her hair caught on something, jerking her head backward. She cried out in pain. He stopped walking and put her down on the ground, gently.

"My fault. I should have picked it up," he said.

He hurried down the length of her hair which was like a lighted rope trailing behind her. He found where it was tangled on a fallen tree branch. He freed it carefully, meticulously, then gathered it in his arms as he walked back toward her. An armful of starlight cradling against him as though it were something precious, something fragile. Something sacred.

Her throat tightened.

The image struck her. The sight of him, this stranger, this storm-fallen guardian, bundling her magic into his arms with quiet reverence undid the tightness in her chest. Affection flooded her.

Her heart thumped once. And for a breathless moment, the forest faded—the trees, the shadows, the danger—and there was only Cassian.

Only this impossible man holding the truth of her in his hands. When he arrived back at her, he held the bundle out to her.

"Thank you," she said as she took it.

And then he picked her up again and started walking, the awkward mass of her hair cradled between them.

"How did they find us?" she asked.

"The moment we landed in Starna, the world remembered you. And the usurper *knew*."

Men's voices floated through the air toward them. He cast a glance over his shoulder, sucked in a sharp breath, and picked up speed. She didn't have to look to know the men on horseback were now following on foot.

"They're coming, aren't they?" she asked, her voice timid.

But he didn't answer. His jaw was set, his eyes sharp with focus. She looked back and saw them. Their torches bobbed through the trees. Figures entered the forest behind them, their firelight clawing through the dark night. She sucked in a deep breath. There was nowhere to hide. Nowhere to go. She wanted to vanish. To pull the shadows and the forest close around them like a cloak.

And then, the air shifted.

The trees stirred.

Branches creaked and moved. Falling down to hide them with foliage. Leaves unfurled in large patterns. Vines lifted from the forest floor like serpents waking from a deep sleep, curling the trunks of trees, stretching out on limbs, as though a living veil.

Shouts came. The torches vanished, plunging them into total darkness.

She gasped.

Cassian halted and half-turned to see.

The forest answered her deepest unconscious request.

He stared into the darkness where the torches vanished. The surrounding forest was quiet now. Waiting. Protecting.

When he looked at her, there was not fear in his eyes but something else. Wonder. Admiration. Awe.

"You made a wish, and the forest obeyed," he said softly.

She opened her mouth to reply but didn't. Couldn't. She didn't know what to say. Finally, she nodded. "I suppose I did."

A smile tugged at the corner of his mouth, pulling one side up. Her gaze fixed on his lips. Lips, she suddenly realized, that were perfect for kissing.

"You are a wonder, my stardust."

Stardust.

She flushed hot at the nickname and tore her gaze away from his.

Sparks of light flashed once and then disappeared. Then flashed again and disappeared. But never in the same place twice. And suddenly there were more and more as they danced around the two of them. His arms tightened on her as he continued to hold her and watched with the same wonder she felt as the flashing light appeared and then disappeared. Appeared and disappeared.

The flutter of wings beat against her cheek. She flinched. But she didn't swat it away.

"What is it?" she asked.

"I'm not sure."

He stepped toward a fallen log and eased her down onto it. Her mass of hair pooled in her lap, glowing faintly in the dark. Firefly-like bulbs flickered all around her. Again, something fluttered against her cheek, light and delicate, like wings. She stilled, watching and waiting. Her breath in her throat.

Then, soft as a petal falling, a creature alighted on the mound of hair in her lap.

The glow from her hair lit the tiny figure no taller than six inches, standing bold and still with sparkling skin that shimmered in the faint light. A sharp chin jutted upward. Long pointed ears poked out from the side of her head. She planted feet shoulder-width apart, hands firmly fisted on her slender hips in an unflinching stance. Iridescent wings blurred behind her, fast as a hummingbird.

The little creature stared up at her with golden eyes as if *she* was the odd one.

"Hello," she said carefully.

The tiny creature narrowed bright eyes. "Took you long enough."

Ariadne blinked. "I'm sorry?"

"I've been circling your glowing head for five minutes, and all I get is 'hello'? You could've offered a hand. Or a snack."

"A snack?" Ariadne echoed, completely thrown.

The creature huffed, crossing her arms. "Do you have any honey drops? Dewberry crumbs? No? Ugh. Mortals."

"I—well, I didn't expect—"

"Clearly." She gestured with one hand at Ariadne's lap. "That is a lot of hair you have there. Very dramatic. Is it always like that or is this a special occasion?"

A small laugh slipped out of Ariadne before she could stop it. She pressed a hand to her forehead. "I think I'm having a strange day."

The tiny, winged girl gave her a knowing smirk. "*You're* having a strange day? Well, what about *me*? There's you and then this...giant of a man carrying you like some delicate flower."

She flushed as Cassian stepped closer, eyes fixed on the tiny girl still standing proudly on the braid in her lap. His hand drifted toward the hilt of his blade.

"Don't speak to it," he said quietly, voice low and tight. "Sylphs are tricksters. They'll charm you with riddles and steal the name from your bones before you know it's gone."

The girl scoffed, utterly unfazed. "*Rude.* Step aside, giant. I'm talking to the girl."

Ariadne looked between them. "She hasn't done anything."

"*Yet*," Cassian muttered. "She hasn't done anything *yet*."

The sylph rolled her eyes with such force it was impressive for someone six inches tall. "Honestly, the dramatics. Do I look like a name-thief? You're thinking of piskies. Ugh. Realm guardians. So uptight."

Ariadne stared down at the small girl with the audacious personality. Unable to stop herself, she smiled. "You know who I am, don't you?"

The sylph beamed. "Of course I do, *Starborn*. The forest told me the moment your braid touched leaves."

Cassian took a step forward. "What do you want from her?"

The tiny girl turned, planted her hands on her hips again, and said, "To help. *Obvy*. Stars above, you people are exhausting."

Ariadne waved him off with a sweep of her hand. "It's all right, Cassian. Maybe she can help."

"Of course, I can!" She fluttered upward, hovering in front of Ariadne's face. "You need a safe place. I can take you there." She thumbed at her chest, the pride of knowing lighting her face.

"I don't think so—"

The girl flew right for Cassian and got in his face. "You don't trust me, do you?"

"Should I?" he asked, calm and cool. His expression remained impassive.

She spun back toward Ariadne. "Do you believe this guy?"

"What's your name?" She tried not to smirk at the exasperation on the sylph's face.

"Twill." She alighted once again on the mound of hair. "And *you* are the lost heir."

Heat flashed through her as she looked up at Cassian whose expression was guarded and wary. He rested his hand on the hilt of his dagger.

"She is," he answered.

"I knew it." Twill bowed low. "Your majesty, welcome to Gloamwood Forest."

"Don't call me that."

She lifted her head. "Then what should I call you?"

"Ariadne."

"Very well, then. Come, Ariadne. And you, too, giant. Despite your mistrust, my people and I will grant you safe passage through the forest."

"Where are you taking us?" Cassian demanded. He helped her to her feet.

"To the wood elves, where else? High Queen Kaylessa will want to meet you."

As the sylph fluttered away, Cassian took her hand in his and squeezed.

"Are you sure about this?" he asked.

"No," she admitted. "But it doesn't seem as though we have much choice."

Nodding, he led her from the fallen log and followed the flickering lights ahead of them through the dark forest.

CHAPTER 7

Ariadne picked her way through the forest floor with delicate steps. When it was too much for her bare feet, Cassian swept her up into his arms again, making her flush. It was far too intimate, but he wasn't flustered by it. Or if he was, he managed to hide it behind his cool façade.

Twill led them through the veiled part of the forest. The trees changed, as though morphing into something else. Taller. Stronger. Wider. Still cloaked in shadow. Paths shifted as they walked through the foliage. Time moved differently here within the woodlands. As though ever-changing with each step they took to get closer to their destination.

"We're passing through the hidden veil," he said, his voice low.

"What is that?" she asked.

Overhead, the canopy of leaves moved and swayed in an invisible breeze.

"It's the barrier that separates the Elven realm," he said.

"That's right," Twill piped up. "It's a hidden realm. Unless you know where to look for it."

Her fluttering body circled their heads. As she flashed by, Ariadne saw joy lighting her face. She was excited to enter this realm of the wood elves deep within Gloamwood Forest.

When they passed through the veil, a shudder of delight went through her, as though all her nerve-endings were tingling with the wonder of magic. She loosed a breath through her lips.

"Are you all right?" he asked, his blue eyes on hers.

"I sensed something as we passed through the veil."

"That's the Elven magic," Twill answered. Her little body bobbed up and down before them. "They know we've entered their realm."

"How do they know that?"

"Elven magic," Cassian said with a hint of a smile.

"If they didn't grant us permission to enter, we wouldn't have been able to pass through the veil," Twill added. "This way."

She veered left, slipping them between two towering ash trees whose trunks bent toward each other. It was not a path, but a gateway. The air changed the moment they went through. Calmer. Quieter. Just a serene stillness.

Above them the canopy parted, revealing a shaft of shimmering light like filtered starlight. It glistened as it beamed down through the cluster of leaves overhead that blotted out the night sky. How was this possible?

The forest opened wider, revealing a sweeping staircase carved from moss-veiled stone, its edges softened by ivy and worn by time. Glowing blossoms clung to the balustrade as through a guide.

At the midpoint stood three figures. Silent. Unmoving. Observant. A tall woman in silverleaf robes stood at the center, her long flowing hair cascading over her shoulders to her waist. On her head, she wore a silver circlet bearing the insignia of the Elves. One glittering jewel sat in the middle of her forehead.

She was flanked by two men. Both of them wore a helm of polished silver and stood tall and straight with hands upon the hilts of their swords.

Their eyes, ageless and ancient, fixed on her. Not with fear or suspicion but with something else. Something far more unsettling.

Recognition.

As they reached the foot of the steps, Cassian settled her to her feet. Twill continued to flitter around her head. Then paused long enough to give a bow of her small body.

"Your majesty, High Queen Kaylessa of the Wood Elves, I present to you Ariadne, the Starborn."

"Can it be true?" Wonder tinged her voice. The queen stepped down to pause in front of her, her gaze still fixed on her. "Is it truly you?"

"I only know what I've been told," she said, then added hastily, "your majesty."

The queen's pale gaze landed on Cassian then. "And you. Who are you?"

"A Guardian of Knowledge, your majesty. I was the one who found the prophecy and brought her from the human realm." He bowed low to her.

She lifted a thin, pale brow. "Through a Celestial Gate?"

"Yes."

"They have closed all the Celestial Gates," the queen said. "How, then, did you return?"

Cassian cast Ariadne a questioning glance. Taking that as her cue, she stepped forward, dropping the mass of her hair. The braid landed in a pool of shimmering light in front of her.

"With my hair," she said.

The queen was silent for a long moment as her pale gaze examined her hair. She reached out as if to touch it, then stopped herself.

"How is it possible?" she whispered.

"One cut strand created an opening. To here," Ariadne said.

"It's true, then?"

"It is." Cassian stepped forward. "She stands before you as the rightful heir to the Starna throne. The one the usurper stole."

The queen of the Elves dropped to her knees then in a deep curtsy. The two guards behind her did the same. Taking a cue from them, Cassian did the same. Twill alighted on the ground, her wings still fluttering as the sylph also bowed. Discomfort moved through her. She hadn't expected this at all.

"Please, you do not need to bow to me," she said.

With her head still low, the queen of the Elves said, "You are the rightful ruler of our realm, my queen. Which means you rule all there is to Starna, including my woodland realm."

"Rise. All of you. I insist."

They all rose. When the Elven queen looked at her, there was an openness about her expression. "You are most welcome here in my kingdom."

"I helped bring her," Twill announced, still fluttering in the air near Ariadne's head.

A smile spread across the queen's face. "You and the guardian are also welcome here. Come."

She motioned toward the stairs behind her, then turned without a word, gliding upward like a moonlit shadow. Ariadne and Cassian fell in step behind her, her bare feet on the cool, moss-covered ground. As they climbed, she caught his glance. His eyes were alert, full of life, with a glint of curiosity.

Twill darted ahead, a blur of iridescent wings and muttering something about a welcome lantern under her breath.

At the top, the trees parted as if bowing and Ariadne halted. Her breath caught in her throat as she looked upward. High above, it was as though the forest bloomed in starlight, reaching for the sky that was nothing more than a blank canvas. No stars. No light. Nothing.

"There are no stars here," she breathed.

"It is the ever-night," Twill said in her ear.

"Ever-night?"

"Since the usurper took control of the realm, the sun has faded into nothing. Only the true heir can bring balance back to our world," Kaylessa said.

And they thought she was the one to do that? A weight pressed against her chest, tightening and making it difficult to breathe. It was a lot for her to accept in a short amount of time.

"Come." Kaylessa waved them forward. "I have a place you can rest and rejuvenate."

Silver-leafed trees spiraled high into the air as they continued to walk through the forest on the moonlit path. They passed shores with crystal-laced streams flowing over moss-covered rocks in such a way that made it sound as though the water sang as it moved. Softly glowing lanterns hung mid-air without string or hooks, pulsing softly like fireflies. A soft breeze carried the scent of jasmine and rain-soaked bark. In the distance, the tinkling of wind chimes made of glass echoed faintly through the trees.

Ariadne had not stepped through a magical forest.

She had stepped into a dream.

The queen led them to the shores where a large hollowed out tree opened to give them the respite they needed. The view was that of the starlight-drenched water, the soft babbling of the river, and the call of a nightbird. Inside the hollowed trunk, worn smooth from time alone, a mound of pillows clustered on a low mattress.

"My servants will attend you," she said. She bowed low and left them there.

Twill immediately went into the hollow tree. She alighted on a large, fluffy pillow that shimmered in the half-light. After fluffing it with her feet, she settled down, curling into a ball. Her wings stopped fluttering and, before long, she was fast asleep.

"Take some rest," Cassian said as he stood near the shores. His hand was on the hilt of his dagger as though he expected trouble.

"What about you?" she asked.

"I'll keep watch." He granted her a smile and motioned toward the pillows. "Rest. We have a long journey yet."

Nodding, Ariadne made her way inside the hollow trunk. After arranging the pillows to her likening, she settled down beneath the tree surrounded by warmth, comfort, and a sense of serenity.

As her eyes drooped, someone arrived. A man. Tall, with a flowing cape behind him. His boots were silver. His pants white and stark. His hair, long and flowing, fluttered behind him. His face held a stern expression as his sharp eyes took in first Cassian, then her.

Cassian moved to stand between the two of them, as though her protector and shield.

"I heard of the Starborn's arrival, and I had to come see for myself."

His voice was sharp, unrelenting, as he peered around Cassian at her. She didn't like the way he looked at her at all.

"I am Cassian, Guardian of Knowledge. And you are?" His voice held quiet authority.

He regarded him with cool disinterest before answering. "Cyran. High Warden of the Woodland Elves."

His unblinking gaze stayed on her. As though she were something of an enigma he didn't wish to figure out.

She rose, spine straightening, as she moved to stand next to Cassian. She lifted her head, chin up, and mustered her courage. "I am Ariadne."

"I know who you are, girl. The Starborn." He sniffed derision. As though the title meant nothing to him. He treated her with disdain, not honor.

A blur of light and wings zipped between them.

Twill.

"You will not speak to her like that, you villainous scallywag," she snapped, clearly agitated by the gruffness of the man. "She is the rightful heir, *your heir,* not some half-wit girl from a foreign land."

He swatted at her as though she were nothing more than a nuisance. She dodged, zipping up to tug a strand of his silver-streaked hair, then zipping away just as quickly.

Cassian's lips twisted at the sylph, but he managed to maintain control of his expression. Ariadne, her heart thudding, brushed her hand against his to draw upon his strength.

"Her majesty has granted you sanctuary. I will abide by her wishes for now." He leaned forward, his suspicious gaze focused on her. "But know this, Starborn. You may carry divine blood, but that does not make you wise. Or welcome."

Then he stalked off, his boots shuffling the grass as he left them.

"You lickspittal strumpet-sired flapdoodle!" Twill shouted after him.

Though it was likely, he never heard a word.

Twill's little body vibrated with all her wrath.

"It's all right, Twill," Ariadne said, hiding her grin at the creative insult the sylph hurled at the back of the warden. "I'm not afraid of him."

"You shouldn't be. You have the queen's protection, after all."

"I think we should all get some rest," Cassian said, trying to diffuse the situation. "I'll keep watch while you two rest."

Twill went back to her fluffy pillow, repeated her ritual, and then, finally, settled down to sleep. Ariadne held back, staring at the space the warden vacated.

"Do you think he'll try to cause trouble for us?" she asked.

"If he does, we will go to the queen. I've no doubt she'll help us."

Nodding, she returned to the mound of pillows and the makeshift bed she created for herself. As she settled down, the last thing she recalled was seeing Cassian's stiff back as he stood watch.

Chapter 8

Cassian stared at the stream, listening to the soft babbling as it tumbled over the moss-covered rocks. The shore stretched as far as he could see on either side, bathed in odd silvery light that did not come from the stars—it came from the leaves. Across from him, darkness settled on the trees making them nothing more than shapes in the shadows.

Here in the Elves woodland world, he felt safe under the watchful care of the queen. But the warden...that man left him unsettled. His haughty derision and suspicious glances he cast at Ariadne did not bode well.

She was right to question him. The warden appeared to want nothing more than trouble. Though what kind, he was unsure.

A servant brought a tray of food with a silver carafe and cups. Pomegranates and figs piled high and surrounded by grapes, bread, slices of cheese, and other fruit. He ate in solitude, keeping a watchful eye on Ariadne and Twill as they slumbered. Ariadne's mass of hair spilled around her and even as she slumbered, the strands pulsed with their exquisite light. As he watched her sleep, he noticed something, too. Her hair—once a tight braid—began to unravel. Perhaps that was simply because of their fall through the star gate and the trek through the forest.

Once they left the security of the Woodland Elves domain, he worried what would happen to them. He was, after all, an outlaw. The other guardians gave their lives so he could enter the human realm. Now that he was back, with Ariadne, it would only be a matter of time before they were discovered by the usurper and his forces.

Well, they were already discovered. The men following them to the forest was proof of that. The usurper, so afraid of losing his throne and his power, must have spelled the sky and the gates to alert him of her imminent return.

But, perhaps, it was something else.

The world around them sensed the heir's return. Even High Queen Kaylessa recognized her. And Twill. The sylph knew her on sight.

He tried to ignore the apprehension sweeping through him, but it was hard to set aside. The heir, his stardust, did not yet know what she was up against. It would be a difficult road to defeat the usurper. She also did not know the gods had prepared her for that. She was stronger than she knew with a resilience buried deep within her bones, within her magic.

As he munched on a fig, he considered all this, all the options. There were no other options other than to take her to the Celestial Gate.

The snap of a twig caught his attention. Queen Kaylessa emerged from the shadows carrying something draped over her arm and a pair of soft boots. No doubt for the heir. She granted him a smile as she approached.

"I brought these things for her," she said. "A hooded cloak made of the finest Elven material. It will help hide her hair. Traveling clothes to give her ease of movement. And these boots."

As he took the offered items, he wondered if Twill asked for them. He hadn't had a chance.

"You're most kind, your majesty, and I thank you for your generosity."

"It was a small thing." She looked toward the sleeping heir and her sylph. "Does she understand the weight she carries?"

"No," he said. "Though I did try to explain it to her."

"She will need your strength, then, guardian." Her eyes flickered back to him. "And something else."

He lifted a brow, unsure what she meant. His head inclined to one side in question. She glanced over her shoulder, her keen eyes scanning the area. Then she stepped closer and dropped her voice.

"There is a sacred relic that lies at the heart of woodland realm. In a glade. Given to us by the gods themselves to guard until such time the Starborn returned."

A tingling sensation skipped up his spine. "What is this sacred relic?"

"A piece of a fallen star said to stabilize the Celestial Gate. Or destroy it if it falls into the wrong hands. This is why the usurper cannot know it's here. He will use it to destroy what's left of our realm. The gods call it a Starshard."

Cassian glanced at Ariadne who slept on. "How does she use it?"

"Only with the magic buried deep inside her can she stabilize the gate and return Starna to its former glory. It is said when the heir returns, the realm will begin to fracture. The usurper will know she has returned and will hunt her until she's dead. Already the gates begin to crack." She reached for him then, placing a hand on his shoulder. "When she wakes, bring her to me. We will go to the glade so she can retrieve it."

"I can wake her now."

"No. Allow her this respite, for once she has the sacred relic, her life will be in continual jeopardy. You must see her safely to the Celestial Gate high above the Elysian Summit. Climb the Whitefire Tower to the tallest turret. There she will use her magic and the relic to reclaim the land by opening the gate."

"What happens when she does?" A sense of foreboding shifted through him.

"The usurper will no longer hold power over Starna."

A warning tinged with hope. He nodded. "I understand."

She dropped her hand and turned away.

"One more question, your majesty. Why did the gods give it to you?"

"Because they knew we would hide it with our Elven magic and guard it with our lives. Bring her when she wakes. We haven't much time left."

He watched her go, his gut churning acid. The queen was right. From here on, the journey would turn treacherous. And it was up to him to keep her safe from those who wanted her dead.

Including, he suspected, the High Warden.

***

Ariadne awoke sometime later, her eyes blinking open to the same pale light surrounding her. There was no sun in this land. Only that ethereal glow from the sky. Her hair wrapped around her like a shimmering cocoon, spilling out onto the ground. The piece she cut to escape the human realm curled downward and rested on her shoulder. It seemed it had grown even in the short time since it was cut.

Turning her head, she saw Twill continued to nap on her fluffy pillow. Her wings were folded against her back. Her knees were tucked against her chest, her slender arms wrapped around them. Watching the sylph sleep made her smile. She looked so serene, so calm, so peaceful. Unlike the flurry of light that followed her when she was awake. Not to mention her sharp tongue.

Recalling how she called the warden a scallywag made her smile.

As she sat up, the pillows shifted around her, making a shuffling noise. Cassian, who remained outside keeping vigil, turned. Their eyes met. His unreadable blue eyes in the shadows. A smile spread as he walked toward her, extending a hand down to her.

"You're awake. Sleep well?"

She took his hand and allowed him to hoist her to her feet. "As well as can be expected, I suppose." She noticed the food tray and headed toward it as her stomach rumbled.

"The queen came while you slept."

She popped a grape in her mouth. "Oh?"

"She brought you these." He extended the clothes and boots to her. "And...a message."

"A message?" She accepted the clothes and boots, grateful to have something to wear if they continued their trek through the forest.

"She asked we meet with her. There is...something she wants to give you."

Ariadne held up the clothes, inspecting them. Padded pants, an oversized tunic, a leather vest, woolen socks, and a hooded cloak.

"What does she want to give me?"

"Eat and change, then I'll take you to her."

He sounded guarded, as though he didn't want to tell her. She snatched up a fig, popping it into her mouth, and headed back to the small alcove in the tree. He turned his back, keeping watch as she slipped on the pants under her gown. Turning away from him she shucked her dress to pull on the tunic and the vest. Then plopped down on the ground to tug on the woolen socks and boots. Everything was a perfect fit. As though made for her. She pulled the cloak around her shoulders, leaving the hood off.

Her movement roused Twill who rubbed her eyes, yawned, and stretched. She gave Ariadne a nod of approval.

"Much better, Starborn. You're ready to take on the realm now."

Ariadne wasn't sure she was ready for that, but she nodded agreement, nonetheless.

Once she was dressed—wearing shoes for the first time in a long while was strange—she followed Cassian from their secluded sanctuary. Twill bounced and fluttered alongside her as they walked through the mystical forest.

As they made their way, they garnered a few curious glances from the other Elves. A few bowed their head in reverence as they passed. Some stared in awe. All the attention made her uncomfortable. She'd spent her youth in solitude with only the caretaker to keep her company.

They arrived at the base of an enormous tree with silvery leaves and moss curling around the trunk. The queen greeted them with a smile.

"You looked rested," she said. Then to Cassian, "Thank you for bringing her. Follow me."

Without waiting for an answer, she darted away. Her two guards flanked her. Cassian, Ariadne, and Twill fell in step behind her.

"Where are we going?" Ariadne asked.

"To the glade," the queen said.

She cast a questioning glance at Cassian, but his face was impassive. Did he know, and he chose not to share it with her? Why were they going to the glade?

He moved closer to her. "I'll explain when we arrive."

He said it as they passed by the warden with his watchful gaze. His eyes were narrowed. He hurried to catch up with the queen, moving to stand in front of her and blocking the path.

"Where are you going, your majesty?" he asked.

"Step aside, Cyran. This does not concern you."

"The safety of this realm *does* concern me. Especially with strangers here." His heated gaze landed on her and Cassian.

Her senses went on high alert. She didn't like this High Warden.

"And I am your queen. They are not strangers. They are our honored guests. You will do as I command. Stand aside and let us pass."

Her two guards rested their hands on the hilts of their swords. Cyran glared at the queen, his eyes lit with indignation. He wanted to retort. His lips twitched with his disdain. His gaze flickered to the guards, then to her and Cassian. Finally, he held his hands up and stepped aside to let them pass.

But something told Ariadne the High Warden was not through with them.

The queen's steps never faltered as she hurried to the edge of the trees. The forest opened into a grove with moonlit drenched grass. A low stone rose in the center. Something glimmered under a dome on top of the stone. The queen led them straight to it and halted, waiting for them to catch up.

Ariadne hurried to it, staring down at the shining object under the dome. It looked like a sliver of glass as it pulsed. The closer she got to it, the more frantic the pulsing. As though it sensed her.

"What is this?" She dropped to her knees to get a closer look.

"Did you not tell her?" The queen asked Cassian.

"Not yet."

Twill alighted on Ariadne's shoulder, her wings fluttering next to her ear. She gasped, the sound quiet. "It's a fallen star."

"A piece of one, yes," Kaylessa said. "It is a sacred relic that was given to us by the gods as a weapon against evil. And it belongs to you, Ariadne."

Her head snapped up to the queen. "Me?"

"With your power and this Starshard, you can unlock the Celestial Gate and free us from the usurper's tyranny," Kaylessa said.

She looked back at the Starshard under the dome, its light pulsing and dancing and shimmering. It was shaped like an elongated rock with one end more narrow than the other which lent itself to a handle. She reached for the dome, placing her hand on the cool glass. The moment she did, the star's power ignited into a bright white flash. It banged against the dome, as though desperate to be free.

"How do I get it?" she asked.

"I do not know," Kaylessa confessed. She looked to Cassian for assistance. "Do you know, Cassian?"

"Her hair is the key, I think," he said. He dropped to his knees next to her. His warmth radiated outward toward her. "Ariadne, remember when you cut your hair to open the portal?"

Understanding dawned as she glanced back at the flickering star under the dome. "Yes," she said slowly.

"Another piece could release the Starshard."

She examined the dome closer. At the bottom, she saw what appeared to be a seal in the shape of a star. It gave her an idea. She pulled her braid over her shoulder, holding the thick hair as she considered the seal and what her hair might do to break it. Rather than cutting a piece, she plucked a short one close to her hairline. She swiped the piece of hair over the seal.

The moment she did, a light burst forth. There was a click and a hiss and suddenly the dome swished open. The star burst toward her and dropped into her lap. She sucked in a breath as she gazed down at the piece of fallen star. It appeared to be nothing more than a jagged piece of rock that shimmered and pulsed with life. She plucked it up from her lap.

"*Ohhh*," Twill said in her ear. "Beautiful."

"What do I do with it?" Ariadne asked.

"You must go to the Elysian Summit at once," Kaylessa urged. "Cassian, you know what to do."

He wrapped a hand around her upper arm and gave her a gentle nudge to stand. As he did, she pocketed the Starshard.

"You do?" Ariadne asked him.

Before he answered, the forest around them fell silent. He thought he heard a swish of leaves, the snap of a twig. The trees swayed. His keen eyes scanned the area.

"What is it?" she whispered, sensing his unease.

"Something is wrong."

As he said it, armed men holding swords or bows emerged from the trees. They were surrounded and outnumbered. And leading them was Cyran, the High Warden. He halted in front of Ariadne, his eyes glittering with loathing.

"You're now a prisoner of his honored majesty, the King of Starna."

"Cyran! What have you done?" Kaylessa glared at him with shock and horror. Her two armed guards moved to stand in front of her to protect her.

"And you, High Queen Kaylessa." He snorted. "You are under arrest for treason."

Her mouth turned down in a sour frown. "*You* are the one committing treason, Cyran. Not me."

"Arrest them all," he ordered.

Twill launched off her shoulder in a blur of wings and right-eous fury.

Ariadne barely had time to gasp before the sylph became a streak of glowing light, shrieking like a tiny war goddess as she hurled herself at the High Warden's face.

The sound was piercing—somewhere between a battle cry and a curse in a language Ariadne didn't know. Cyran recoiled, swatting wildly, but Twill darted and spun too fast to catch. Her wings kicked up sparks as she zipped past his ear again and again.

The distraction worked.

Movement exploded around her. Kaylessa's guards lunged forward, steel flashing in the filtered light as they intercepted the enemy soldiers creeping too close. Blades clashed. Boots slammed against the ground. The air filled with the sharp, singing chaos of battle.

Ariadne's heart surged. Twill had bought them seconds. And in moments like this, seconds were everything.

Cassian's grip on her arm tightened. He yanked her back from the stone, pulling her behind him as two of the High Warden's men charged from the side. With his free hand, he drew his dagger in one fluid motion, the blade flashing in a wide warning arc as he intercepted them.

Ariadne's heart pounded against her ribs. Somewhere behind them, a sharp shout tore through the air, but she didn't dare look. Something hissed past her ear—an arrow, fast and deadly, splitting the air with a shrill whistle before embedding in the stone inches from where she'd been standing.

She barely registered it because in the next breath, Cassian jerked.

Not from the arrow.

From the blade now buried in his shoulder.

"No!" she gasped, reaching for him, but he staggered, releasing her arm as pain overtook him.

Blood bloomed across his tunic.

Before she could even process it, rough arms closed around her from behind. She was hauled off her feet, dragged backward. Cassian tried to lunge for her, but another guard seized him. Then another. He was outnumbered.

One of the men ripped the dagger from his shoulder. Cassian didn't scream, but the way his body buckled said enough.

"Cassian!"

Her cry cracked the air, but he didn't hear. And she was being taken.

"Bring her to me!" Cyran ordered. "We need her magic!"

The man dragged her to the High Warden. She tried digging in her heels into the soft ground, but to no avail. Someone—she assumed Cyran—grabbed her braid and jerked her head back. He put a blade against it.

"Hold her still, man," he ordered.

She struggled in his arms, trying to ignore the pain in her scalp as he pulled her hair. A buzzing surged by her face. Twill? She wasn't certain.

Then she felt a low humming coming from her pocket. *The Starshard.* Fumbling, she managed to retrieve it, closing her fingers around it. When she brought her hand out her pocket, light seeped through her enclosed fingers.

The man's shriek split the air, his grip loosening just enough. She twisted hard—desperate, gasping—and slipped free.

Cyran's voice bellowed behind her, rough with rage. She barely had time to register it before someone slammed into her from the side. The breath whooshed from her lungs as she hit the ground, hard. Hands pinned her shoulders, heavy and unrelenting.

The Starshard tumbled from her fingers, landing in the grass inches away, glinting faintly like it knew what was coming.

Then a sharp yank on her braid. Her head snapped back, pain lancing through her scalp.

"Hold her steady!" Cyran barked. "This is for his majesty, the king."

She couldn't see him, but she felt the danger, the intent behind the command. Her pulse roared in her ears.

A burst of light. The fallen star flared. So did her braid.

A flash of heat surged through her, through the strand anchored to her skull. The man behind her screamed and tore his hand away, smoke curling from his fingers.

A blinding burst of starlight erupted across the clearing. Searing, brilliant, pulsing.

Then silence. A stunned, breathless silence. As if the entire forest had stopped to witness her blaze.

Overhead, a crack followed by a boom that rose and rose and rose to a great crescendo. Beneath her, the earth rumbled. She flipped over in time to see sparks of lightning shoot across the sky in a brilliant arc.

"Duck!" the queen shouted.

Kaylessa and her men fell to the ground, covering their heads. Ariadne didn't understand what she saw, what was happening.

A shuffling of the grass near her caught her attention. Cassian crawled to her, his face pale, and his tunic soaked in blood. He reached a hand toward her but then collapsed.

"No!" The word tore from her throat as she scrambled to him, her limbs shaking, her heartbeat a thunderous roar in her ears. She pulled him into her lap, clutching his body close to hers.

"You're all right," she whispered, frantic. "You're going to be all right, do you hear me?"

His body trembled against hers, and then his voice, weak but steady. "Take the Starshard, stardust. Get to the Elysian Summit."

She was already shaking her head, fiercely, desperately. "No. Not without you. I *won't* do this without you."

"You can."

His eyes fluttered closed.

"No." Her voice cracked. Her hands were slick with his blood, but she held him tighter. "Cassian, please. I didn't want to believe in fate or prophecy or any of this—"

Her voice broke.

"—but I do believe in *you*. Stay with me. Please, stay."

Her head snapped up, heart pounding in her throat. The glade lay in ruin. Bodies were strewn like broken dolls. Limbs twisted, faces slack, blood soaking into the earth. Smoke clung to the edges of the clearing, tinged with the sharp, metallic scent of magic and fire.

She looked to the grass where the Starshard pulsed with celestial light, untouched. Waiting.

Across the carnage, her eyes locked with the High Queen's. The regal calm was gone. Only shock remained.

Ariadne's voice cut through the quiet. "He needs help. Now."

The queen blinked as if yanked from a trance. Then turned to her guards with a crisp command. "See to him. Get him to the village, quickly."

"I'll find the healer!" Twill burst into a streak of furious light and zipped away with a trail of sparks, her tiny voice muttering something that sounded suspiciously like, "If the giant dies, I'll curse every leaf in this forsaken forest..."

The guards moved, lifting Cassian's limp form between them. Ariadne's hands trembled as she wrapped her fingers around the shard. Its warmth pulsed in her palm—soft, insistent, alive.

She tucked it into the pocket of her cloak, held it close to her heart. And followed, whispering silently with every step.

Don't let him leave me.

CHAPTER 9

Twill made good on her promise to find the healer. He was waiting for them when they arrived back in the Elven village. All the way there, Ariadne kept on the lookout for the High Warden, the man who had betrayed her and the High Queen. But he was nowhere. She had never experienced such fury over his betrayal.

The guards took Cassian to the sanctuary they previously occupied and placed him gently on the pile of pillows she had slept on not long ago. The healer went to work on his shoulder, staunching the flow of blood and bandaging him. He gave him something for the pain and to help him rest. Ariadne and the High Queen waited together as the healer finished his work.

"He'll be fine," he announced. "He will heal as he sleeps."

"Thank you, Valys," the High Queen said with a bow of her head.

"Yes, thank you for helping him," Ariadne added.

He nodded, leaving the two of them. Twill settled on her fluffy pillow next to Cassian's head while he slept. She drew her knees up and wrapped her arms around her legs as though keeping vigil.

"I'm sorry about Cyran," the High Queen said. "I didn't know about him."

"Don't apologize." She turned to her, took her hands in hers and gave them a quick squeeze. "It's not your fault."

"I should have realized. I should have known he was a sympathizer of the usurper," she insisted. Frustration creased her face as she released her hands and paced the small area.

"You couldn't have," Ariadne replied. "Where is he now?"

"My men are searching for him. When he's found, he will be punished." Her gaze drifted to the sleeping form of Cassian. "My healer is right. He will be fine when he wakes."

"You said he knew what to do once I had the Starshard," Ariadne said. She stuck her hand in her pocket, wrapping her fingers around the piece of fallen star. The jagged edge bit into her palm. It gave her peace of mind to know it was still there.

"He does. I told him while you were sleeping." A little grin tipped the corners of her mouth. "And now I will share that with you."

The High Queen told her of the Celestial Gate, the Elysian Summit, and the Whitefire Tower. The names echoed through her, as though a memory resurfaced. They were places she had only read about in her books back in the tower in the human realm. Places that were nothing more than myths and legends. But they weren't, were they? They were *real*.

She stared at the High Queen, her breathing shallow. Her heart throbbed a wicked beat. Her nerves were still jangling. She felt as though she stood on the edge of a dangerous precipice.

A gate between realms. A summit touched by starlight. A tower where gods once walked. This was her destiny.

"I didn't want to believe," she said, her voice quiet. The Starshard hummed in her pocket. "Now, I have no choice."

"In the glade, when the ground rumbled and lightning split the sky…" The queen paused, took a deep breath. "That was the Celestial Gate shuddering. It *knows* you're here. And it knows you have the Starshard."

Her hands curled into fists. It was all too much, too fast. Too much to believe. Too much to understand. Hard to contemplate she was the living, breathing prophecy meant to heal a shattered realm.

"We have waited twenty years for your return. The return of light and hope to our realm. I cannot imagine how difficult this is for you," she said.

Ariadne wanted to cry. To scream. To run away.

But she didn't. She stood her ground, straightened her spine, and looked the queen in the eye.

"I am ready to face my fate. Tell me how to get to the Whitefire Tower."

"It is a dangerous trek over the land. You must be prepared. And you must be cautious."

A shout from one of her men interrupted them. The High Queen rushed to greet him. Turning back to Ariadne, she said, "They've found him."

Ariadne didn't know if that was an invitation, but she took it as one. Knowing Cassian and Twill would be safe there, she followed the High Queen from the sanctuary to the center of the village. Two of her men held the High Warden between them. His hands were shackled in front of him. Dirt and blood smudged his torn clothes. Defiance plastered on his face, his head held high. When his gaze landed on Ariadne, his eyes narrowed to slits. He was not pleased to see her there.

Ariadne steeled her nerves, refusing to be intimidated by this man.

A crowd of curious onlookers gathered, their whispers of conspiracy rippling through them.

Kaylessa halted in front of him, her hands fisted at her sides as she glared at him.

"High Warden Cyran, you stand accused of high treason, an act punishable by death. How do you plead?"

"Not guilty," he said, his voice strong and sure. He held his head high, unapologetic.

As though he was confident he had done nothing wrong.

Silence descended as the queen considered his answer. A brow lifted to her hairline, though her face made no other expression.

"You plead not guilty to treason, yet it is an undeniable fact you tried to capture the true heir." She motioned toward Ariadne.

"You can't prove anything," he said.

Outraged, the words burst from Ariadne before she stopped to think. "You tried to kill Cassian. You tried to cut my hair to use it for your own gain. We all saw what you did. We need no other proof than that."

Her braid, resting over her shoulder, shimmed as if in response to this. In her pocket, the Starshard hummed.

His glittery eyes landed on her. "The rightful heir to Starna sits upon the throne. I will fight until my last dying breath to keep him there."

"You admit working with him and his forces, then?" the High Queen asked.

He ignored her question. "This girl is nothing but an imposter."

Suddenly, a blur of light streaked past Ariadne, past the High Queen, and got into the face of the High Warden. Buzzing. Fluttering.

"You lie! Her hair is proof of her noble blood. It was written in the stars by the gods themselves!"

Twill again. She practically dive bombed the face of the High Warden who flinched and tried to get away from the sylph by ducking. The tiny girl was Ariadne's biggest advocate, and she loved her for it.

"Get it away from me!" Cyran shrieked as he jerked backward. The guards tightened their grip on his arms to keep him from bolting.

"Twill," Ariadne called, her voice calm and cool.

The sylph abandoned her attack and returned to her, landing on her shoulder.

"We cannot banish you," Kaylessa said. "Therefore, we have no choice but to imprison you. There, you will await your death sentence. Take him away."

As the guards shoved him into step, he shouted back at them.

"You can imprison me, High Queen, but the usurper knows the girl is here. He *knows* the Starshard has been released from its bonds. He will never stop hunting her!"

A shiver of fear ran down Ariadne's spine as the man's voice faded into oblivion. Her hands were still clenched at her side. She took a deep breath and released it to calm her ragged nerves.

The crowd dissipated as the High Warden was led away, leaving only her, the High Queen, and a few of her guards.

"I can't do this," she whispered, forgetting Twill was on her shoulder.

"You can, Starborn. It's your divine destiny."

Ariadne never believed in destinies. She believed in self-reliance. It was all she had those lonely years in the tower with nothing but books and the restless stars overhead to keep her company. Now, she faced an impossible choice. Embrace her destiny as the daughter of the gods, the ones who created her out of love to protect the realm of Starna and lead it out of darkness.

Kaylessa turned to her then, her face drained of color as she realized the gravity of the situation.

"I'm afraid he's right. The usurper will hunt you until the end."

Ariadne didn't know who the usurper was or why he was so dangerous. There was nothing in her tower books to give her this information. All she really knew was what Cassian told her about her lineage.

"Who is this usurper?"

Twill sucked in a breath. Kaylessa's face remained impassive. She clenched her jaw tight, then glanced around to see if there were others listening.

"I will not speak of his treachery here. Come with me."

"I shouldn't. Cassian—"

"I'll look after him." Twill hurried off before she replied as though she were afraid to hear the story of the usurper.

The High Queen led her from the center of the village to the base of a tree where a staircase spiraled its way upward. At the top, she led her across a walkway and through an opening in the trees. As they entered, a veil of silvery leaves dropped down to hide them from view.

It was a small, modest house. Nothing ostentatious for this High Queen. In the center, a table with four chairs. Beyond that in an alcove, a four-poster bed piled high with pillows and a thick mattress. Other seating was a wooden two-seat sofa, one cush-ioned chair, a low table between them. The floors were wood, covered in a plush garnet rug.

Kaylessa motioned to the table in the center where she pulled out a chair. Ariadne took the seat across from her.

Fatigue lined her soft features. She rested her hands on the top of the table as she sat back in the chair and regarded her.

"You truly do not know?" she asked.

Ariadne shook her head.

"Then I will tell you the story. Bastion was descended from a long line of noble stewards. They were an ancient line devoted to the protection of Starna and granted immense power for their unwavering loyalty to the realm.

"As the realm flourished, so did his resentment of his role as a servant. He believed he should be able to forge his own path, not follow one dictated by the gods. His hunger for com-plete power twisted into something dark, something desperate, something evil.

"He led a rebellion from within and struck down the ruling family—his. He killed them one by one. He claimed the Whitefire Tower and seized control of the Celestial Gate. He maintained control of the realm through fear and manipulation. Too late the gods realized what was happening. The usurper was beyond their control, their reach. And so, they created the Starborn Child and secreted her away from Starna until such time came for her to regain control of the realm. For only she has the power to break the dark hold he has on the Celestial Gate."

Kaylessa didn't have to tell her she was the Starborn Child. That she understood completely.

"The Celestial Gate at the Whitefire Tower?" she asked.

"Yes." The queen's voice was soft, but the weight behind it hit like a stone. She leaned in across the table, her eyes ancient and unblinking. "You are the last hope, Ariadne. Not a myth. *You*."

Ariadne's breath caught. Her mouth went dry.

"If you refuse…" The queen exhaled hard and sat back, the strength draining from her. "Then we are already lost."

The words lodged deep, burrowing under her ribs. Ariadne stared at her hands, curled tight in her lap. She didn't feel like a savior. She didn't even feel real.

How was she supposed to do this?

All her life, she'd read tales about chosen ones—brave girls, wild-hearted boys, impossible quests. But none of those stories had felt like this. None of them had been her. And yet here she was. In the heart of an ancient realm, with a queen calling her the last hope of a dying world.

She stood slowly, hands trembling. "Thank you for telling me."

Thin, weak words. Words that pulsed with the weight in her chest. She turned, the curtain of silvered leaves parting slightly as she reached for the edge. She needed air. Space. Anything that didn't feel like fate pressing down on her.

"Ariadne."

The queen's voice stopped her.

"I know the task sounds insurmountable," she said gently. "But...will you try?"

Ariadne glanced back. The queen's gaze held hers—steady, unyielding, and impossibly kind. There was no judgment there. But there was hope. It pierced straight through her.

Her throat tightened.

"I don't know what I'm capable of," she said quietly. "But I'll consider what you've said."

And for now, that was the bravest thing she could give.

She headed back to the sanctuary where Cassian rested and Twill watched over him. She did not own the stalwart heart of the sylph. She was a formidable foe, and an ally Ariadne was glad to have on her side. Thinking of her made her smile.

When she arrived, Cassian was sitting upright. His face was pale, but other than that he appeared better. His eyes were sharp and assessing as she came face to face with him. Joy lit through her. She hurried to his side, dropping to her knees next to him and reaching for his hand.

Twill remained on her fluffy pillow next to the guardian.

"Told you I'd watch over him," she said. She folded thin arms over her puffed out chest, proud of her accomplishment.

"A fine job she did, too," Cassian said. "She chattered my ear off."

She snickered. "You look better. How are you feeling?"

"Much better. Strong enough to walk." He shifted as though ready to stand and get on with their quest. Sucking in a breath, he winced as he fell back into the pillows.

"You're not ready, yet."

And neither was she.

"I have to be ready. The realm cannot wait," he said.

Apprehension swept through her as she thought of leaving the silvery shores of the Elven realm. She released his hand and sat back on one of the pillows, careful not to disturb Twill's smug satisfaction.

"The High Warden was apprehended," she said. "And then the High Queen and I spoke."

Curiosity glinted in his eyes. "Oh?"

"She told me about the usurper and how he came to power. Why did you not?"

"I wanted to," he admitted. He looked away, keeping his eyes downcast. "The most important thing was getting you here."

"And meeting me," Twill chirped.

Cassian rolled his eyes.

"I saw that!" She *hmphed* and turned her back on them, plopping down on the pillow once more. Her wings fluttered in agitation.

Ariadne grinned at the sylph's indignation, then turned serious. She wanted to reach for his hand again, to touch him, to draw from his strength, but she refrained. "I don't know if I can do this, Cassian. I'm not a savior. Just a girl."

He lifted his eyes to hers. She saw within the depths confidence. *In her.* And it unnerved her. Reaching for her, it was his turn to take her hand and hold it. His thumb swept over her knuckles.

"You were built to be a savior, stardust."

"You sound sure about that," she said.

"I am." He granted her a knee-melting smile that warmed her from the inside out.

"I can't do this alone."

"You aren't alone." He tugged her closer, leaning toward her. His nose brushed hers. "You have me."

"But there is so much...despair. So much darkness."

He leaned in until their foreheads touched, the space between them vanishing like mist at dawn. His voice, low and reverent, curled around her like a vow spun from moonlight.

"Your light shines brighter than the most luminous star in the sky," he murmured. "There is no darkness with you, stardust. And I will follow you no matter what."

The words struck something deep inside her, fragile and fierce all at once.

She couldn't breathe.

His closeness scattered her thoughts like leaves whirling in the wind. Her heart was pounding, wild and uneven, fluttering in her chest as quick as Twill's wings. He was so near. Too near. Not near enough.

Stars, I like him.

It wasn't just the way he looked at her like she mattered. It was the way he saw her—not as the Starborn, not as the prophecy, but as a girl craving acceptance, belonging, and friendship.

"You mean that?" she whispered, afraid to hope, more afraid not to.

His eyes gazed into hers with such deep affection, it nearly made her come undone. "You have my solemn vow."

Then his lips brushed hers, soft and deliberate, the barest whisper of contact. It wasn't a kiss. Not really. But it stole her breath, anyway. Warmth bloomed beneath her skin, a quiet explosion that lit her up from the inside.

She wanted more.

She couldn't want more.

Her cheeks flamed as she pulled back, heart tripping over itself. And then, Twill's voice cut through the silence.

"The stars don't wait for permission to burn, Starborn."

Ariadne blinked, swallowing the lump in her throat, still caught in the promise of affection.

Wishing for something and claiming it were two different things. And she wasn't sure the stars would wait for her, either.

She let out a shaky breath, grounding herself in Cassian's strength and resolve. She looked toward the shores, where that odd light glistened on the indigo waters as it babbled over rocks and splashed against the shore.

Kaylessa was right. The usurper would never stop hunting her. Did that mean she should hide herself away forsaking all that she was born to do? The longer she delayed, the more treacherous the path to the Celestial Gate would become.

"I don't know what awaits at the Elysian Summit or in the Whitefire Tower. I don't know how to repair the Celestial Gate," she murmured. "But I'm going to get there. I'm going to do what I was born to do. I have to."

Cassian reached for her hand again and squeezed it. Pride glowed in his face. He was honored by her.

"And you won't face it alone."

Twill sighed dramatically from her fluffy pillow. She turned back to face them, her wings still flickering agitation behind her, and her hands propped on her slender hips.

"All right, lovebirds. We have stars to chase and prophesies to fulfill. Not to mention an usurper with a bad attitude and worse hair hot on our heels."

"We? You're coming with us, now?" Cassian asked.

"Yes, giant, I'm coming with you. Don't try to stop me." She wagged a finger at him.

A soft laugh escaped Ariadne. "Of course, you're coming. I wouldn't dream of leaving you behind."

Releasing his hand, she rose, brushing her hand down the length of her glowing braid. It was her greatest legacy and her ultimate weapon. The starlight within it shimmered faintly, as though it, too, was ready.

Cassian got to his feet, smoothing his hands down his tunic. He reached for the hood of her cloak and pulled it up, tucking her hair into the folds to hide it. Well, as much as was possible. There were still strands sticking out around the edges.

"There. That should help. Are you ready?"

Ariadne took a deep cleansing breath, ready to say goodbye to the Elven realm and face her truth. She nodded.

"As I'll ever be."

CHAPTER 10

They bid farewell to the High Queen. Though she was unable to offer any of her men to accompany them, she armed Cassian with a sword made of the finest Elven steel. When she offered Ariadne the same, she declined. She wasn't sure she had the skills to wield a sword. Instead, Cassian gave her his dagger, not wanting her to be unarmed.

Kaylessa gave them each a waterskin.

They started their trek away from the silvery shores of the Elven realm. Ariadne patted her pocket to make sure the Starshard was secure. It wasn't long before they passed through the forest. Before them, the road was long, winding, and desolate.

Twill chattered about anything and everything. A nonstop hum that followed Ariadne. When the sylph tired of flying, she alighted on her shoulder. She perched there which made Ariadne nervous. She had to constantly remind herself she had a passenger.

Cassian was quiet on their trek. Ariadne felt as though the connection they formed in the Elven forest was lost, somehow. It nagged her just as other questions nagged her.

"What's to become of me, Cassian, when all this is done?" she asked.

He gave her a sideways glance. "What do you mean?"

"I mean when Starna is released from the usurper's grasp. What happens to me then?"

"You'll rule the realm, Starborn," Twill answered.

He pressed his lips together at the sylph's response. It told Ariadne that was his answer, as well. It sent a dart of panic to her chest, making it tighten. She pressed a hand there as her breathing grew shallow. She came to a halt in the middle of the road bathed in that odd light from the dark clouds.

"I don't know how to rule."

Cassian wrapped his arms around her, pulling her into his warm embrace. The moment he did, Twill surged off her shoulder and fluttered in the air above their heads. "It's nothing to be worried about yet."

"But—"

"Shh. Don't, Ari. It will only cause you unnecessary worry."

His presence reassured her more than his words. She found comfort in his arms. He also gave her a new nickname—Ari. She liked it. She liked he was comfortable enough to do that with her.

"Where will you go after?" she asked.

"After?"

"When we win?"

"When?" There was a smile in his voice. "Not if?"

She tipped her head back to look up at him. His features were bathed in the blue-white light of the realm, softening them. And she realized then how handsome he was. How he looked at her with the utmost respect and something softer. Something she was not equipped to acknowledge. Butterflies erupted in her stomach.

"I have to believe in when, not if." She rested her head on his shoulder.

They stood in each other's arms in the middle of the road as though this was the most natural thing to do. As though they were not travelers on a quest to reclaim the rule of the realm, but rather lovers stopping for an intimate moment.

"I suppose I'll return to being a Guardian of Knowledge at the Temple of Silence."

That didn't sit right with her. The thought of being parted when the realm was safe sent a pang of sadness through her. She didn't want to be parted from him.

"Head's up, giant!" Twill's warning got their attention.

He released her and stepped back, his hand on the hilt of his sword. She reached for the dagger at her side. In the distance, men on horseback were closing.

"Run!" Twill said.

She was nothing more than a streak of light as she hurried ahead of them. Cassian grabbed her by the hand and broke into a run. She was relieved she had on boots as they hurried down the road.

"What do we...do?" she panted.

Before he answered, Twill was back in front of them, flying backwards. "There's a town ahead. We can take cover there."

"But what if...there are the king's men there, too?" she said.

Cassian never slowed his gait. "How far, Twill?"

"Not far. Follow me and hurry!"

She was off again, forging ahead of them as their guiding beacon bobbed up and down in the space ahead of them. She veered to the right which took them off the main path and plunged them into tall, brittle grass. Something whizzed over their heads, narrowly missing them but headed right for the sylph.

"Twill!" Ariadne gasped.

She dodged as the arrow plunged through the grass, thunking in the ground somewhere near them.

"That was close," Cassian said on a breath.

Too close, she thought. The first sign of the town came into view. Orbs of light dotted the horizon indicating life. Relief spread through her as they approached, knowing they were getting closer.

"We're almost there," Twill announced, her voice high and tinny.

The town loomed ahead. Cassian slowed to a trot, stealing a glance over his shoulder. He came to a halt.

"They're taking the road," he said.

Ariadne followed his gaze to see three men on horseback headed away from them. "Let's hope they don't go into the town."

"Oh, they will," Twill said. "They're heading there, too."

"Then we best find someplace to lie low until we can get out and head to the summit." He took her hand and led her to the edge of the grass.

"How far is the summit?"

"Just over the next ridge," Cassian said. "Another day. Maybe two."

"How did those men find us?" she asked.

"I'm sure our friend Cyran sent messages to every corner of the realm announcing your arrival." There was a bitterness in his voice.

She felt that, too. She hated the man had betrayed not only her, but his own people.

They made it through the open gate. Armed men stood in the towers flanking either side, their burnished armor gleaming faintly with runes that pulsed like slow heartbeats. The guards' eyes glowed faintly amber, enchanted to see through illusion. Ariadne pulled her hood down closer to conceal her face, hoping they were not the king's men.

A narrow cobble street greeted them, winding through to the market square. Lanterns strung overhead flickered not with flame, but with ever-burning starlight—each one encased in floating crystal that shimmered faintly when passed beneath. Several public buildings lined the square. A town hall with ivy that rearranged its leaves to form the time of day, a church with bells that chimed harmonics in a tongue she didn't know, a hall of justice wrapped in weathered stone etched with ancient warding sigils.

Crowds and horses bustled through the streets. Vendors hawked enchanted goods alongside mundane ones. Floating ink pots, cloaks that shimmered with glamours, charms that sang when touched. Tradesmen wandered from booth to booth trying to sell their wares.

Twill dropped from the sky and landed on her shoulder with a satisfied chirp.

"Stick close," Cassian murmured.

Ariadne stepped up her pace and slipped her hand into his. His fingers tightened on hers, grounding her. He seemed to know exactly where they were going, guiding her through the throngs as though he'd walked this path a hundred times. She scanned the crowd, searching for any sign of the men who might have followed them. But the townsfolk seemed unbothered by the state of the realm under the tyrant's rule. They carried on, as if enchantments and oppression were both part of ordinary life.

At the local tavern, Cassian pushed open the heavy wooden door, its surface carved with an old protective charm—a sunburst design worn smooth by time. Inside was a cacophony of sound. A bard sang an old ballad accompanied by a lute that strummed itself on occasion, even as his fingers rested. Laughter rose from shadowed corners. The hum of voices blended with the soft fizz of charmed bottles that never ran dry. Glasses clinked. A barmaid wove through the crowded room, balancing a tray loaded with fresh bread, herb-dusted cheese, and tankards of ale that shimmered faintly with whatever spell kept them perfectly chilled.

Cassian didn't pause. He led her through the tavern to a shadowed corner table along the far wall, where flickering candlelight danced despite the absence of any breeze. He took the seat facing the door, ever vigilant. Ariadne slipped into the seat beside him. Twill fluttered to the tabletop and perched on the edge, eyes gleaming with curiosity.

"Best keep that hood up and your hair covered," Cassian said quietly.

She nodded. Judging by the patrons, many cloaked, some with sigils stitched into their coats or glowing softly at their wrists, it looked like a rough crowd. Perhaps more than human.

The barmaid hurried over. Her appearance was worn thin, tendrils of hair escaping her bun like frayed threads of magic. Her apron bore a faint shimmer, likely warded against minor hexes or spilled charms.

"What'll it be?" she asked, voice flat, eyes sharp as cut stone.

"Stew and ale for all of us," Cassian said.

Then she hurried off without acknowledging his request, disappearing into the crush of people. Cassian leaned back in his chair, his demeanor stiff. His hand landed on the hilt of his sword.

"What is it?" she asked, sensing his unease.

Twill lifted off from the table, her fluttering wings a blur. Then she dropped back down to the table. "We've been made."

"What?" The word came out a roughened whisper.

"I'll handle this," Cassian said. "No talking, Twill."

"But—"

"I mean it," he interrupted.

She frowned and folded her arms over her chest.

A man with a limp approached, his silver eyes resting first on Cassian, then on Ariadne, and finally on Twill, lingering long enough to make her wings twitch. As though he were taking stock not of who they were, but what they were. He smelled of damp earth and smoke, and his long robes appeared to be woven from root and moss, rustling with unseen movement. His hair was wild, his beard reaching his belt in tangled ropes, and his aged face was a map of wisdom carved in lines and shadow.

No weapons. No threat she could see. But everything in Ariadne tensed.

He stopped in front of them and inclined his head. "Starborn. Guardian. Sylph of the Gloamwood. You've come farther than most."

Cassian surged to his feet, his sword half pulled from its scabbard. The overhead candlelight winked against the steel. "Who are you? What do you want?"

A smile played upon his gray lips. "I am friend. Not foe. Put away your weapon, guardian." He motioned to the empty seat then. "May I?"

"Depends," Cassian said. His hand gripped the hilt so tight, his knuckles leached of color.

The stranger cocked his head to one side. Amusement danced in his silver eyes. "On?"

"Your name and the nature of your business."

"Eldrin the Wise, they call me," he replied.

Cassian released his hold on the sword and dropped his hand. "You're a wizard."

He chuckled as he pulled out the chair and sat, not waiting for Cassian to grant his permission. Perhaps, Ariadne mused, a wizard did not need permission.

His gaze turned to Twill. He reached inside the pocket of his robe and brought out a tiny item clearly meant for her. It was hard to see in the low light of the room.

"Your magic is wild, little flame. Let no one cage it."

Twill was on her feet in an instant accepting the gift. "A ring?"

"An Unbinding Ring. Forged between twilight and mist. Offering you protection from those who would cage your wild spirit without your consent. When the time is right, you'll know how to use it."

She scoffed. But even as she did, her hand trembled when she slipped the little ring on the forefinger of her left hand.

Eldrin reached into his other pocket and brought out his fisted hand. He extended it to Ariadne. When he gave her an expectant nod, she held out her hand. He dropped the item into her palm. The cool glass pendant landed. Inside a tear-dropped shaped vial with a cork shimmered a silver thread coiled into a tight spiral. Though it appeared delicate, it hummed and glowed reminding her of humming and glowing stars.

"The stars whisper, but they do not command. You are not the braid, child. You are the loom. When the world insists there is only one way forward, let this remind you that your light was born to choose another."

She peered down at the pendant in awe. It was the most beautiful thing she'd ever seen. She slipped it around her neck.

Eldrin turned to Cassian then. He held a bronze medallion with edges worn smooth in the palm of his hand, though Ariadne hadn't seen how he produced it. It simply appeared. The medallion had a star-spun spiral in the center and hung from a leather cord frayed at the ends.

"This once belonged to a Guardian who chose love over duty. It burns with that choice still. Speak your truth into it, and it will hold you to this world. Not as prisoner, but as partner."

Cassian hesitated before he finally reached for the medallion. He ran his thumb over the star-spun spiral, his gaze full of wonder. He dropped it over his head, letting it rest against his chest. The bronze medallion gleamed in the candlelight.

Eldrin, looking well pleased with his gifts, rose from the table. He gave them all one last glance, a smile playing upon his lips.

"Before I depart, I give you this, Starborn. The gods wove the braid, yes. But it is your soul that binds the magic. Without your choice, the gate will remain closed. You must sever not the strand, but your fear."

Cryptic words she didn't really understand. Her brows drew together. She started to ask another question when he turned to leave.

"Wait!" Ariadne leapt to her feet, her heart beating wildly. Her chair scraped against the wood floor with her sudden movement. She had questions. She didn't want him to get away so quickly.

He turned back, giving her a curious glance over his shoulder.

She asked the first thing that came to mind. "How did you know we were here?"

"Magic draws to magic, child. Like river to sea. Like stars to sky. When prophecy stirs, the world listens."

He melted into the crowd the same way he appeared. Gone in an instant as though swallowed by the shadows. She stood rooted in place and stared at the space he vacated. If she didn't know any better, she'd swear it was all a dream, but for the pendant around her neck.

"Well," Twill said on a breath. "That was weird."

"No," Cassian replied. "That was a wizard."

"Are we *sure* we should have accepted these gifts? Maybe I should toss mine in the river," Twill said.

Ariadne sank to her chair. As she did, the barmaid returned with their order as though nothing had ever transpired. She plunked the tankards and the bowls of stew onto the table with a thud and then took off to tend the other customers without a word.

Cassian reached for a tankard, pulling it toward him. The foam sloshed over the edge and dripped down the side. Twill was interested in one of the bowls of stew. She perched on the edge as though ready to dive in, eyeing one of the large potatoes.

"What did it all mean?" Ariadne asked.

"He means for us to use these gifts at the gate," Cassian said quietly, his voice heavy with unspoken meaning.

Ariadne watched him absently stir the contents of his bowl, then spear a too-perfect round carrot with the spoon. Steam curled up around them, the tavern fire snapping nearby. It should've felt comforting.

It didn't.

Twill, arms crossed and wings twitching, marched across the table with her usual flair. "Well, I'm not using mine," she declared, chin high like a queen of thistle and sass. She planted herself beside Cassian's bowl, golden eyes hopeful as she stared up at him.

Cassian sighed, lowering the spoon in an offering. Twill broke off a piece of carrot and bit into it with dramatic flair. "Mm. Acceptable."

Ariadne stared at the pendant resting below her collarbone, fingers curling around the delicate glass. The thread inside shimmered faintly. Her stomach coiled tight.

"What did he mean?" she asked. "About severing my fear not my braid? How do I even begin to do that?"

Twill licked her fingers and shrugged, wings flicking behind her. "It means you stop quaking in your boots when the sky starts to fall." She popped the rest of the carrot into her mouth and grinned. "Put aside your fear, darling. The Gate only opens for the brave."

Ariadne blinked. That sounded far too confident for someone who'd threatened to fling her gift into a stream not ten minutes ago.

Cassian reached across the table, his fingers brushing hers. Just lightly. Steadying. "You don't have to be fearless," he said, voice low. "Just willing."

She swallowed hard, throat tight. Willing. She could do that. Maybe.

Probably. She hoped.

Twill sighed. "Stars help us all."

It was hard for Ariadne to forget what the wizard said. What did it mean? She did not deny the apprehension sweeping through her at what was to come. Nor did she relish the idea of using the pendant in whatever capacity the wizard deemed. Was it some sort of spell he said as he passed the gifts to each of them?

She caught Twill hovering over her tankard, slurping the last of the lukewarm ale. Twill wiped her mouth with the back of her tiny hand and smirked. "What? Courage needs fortification."

"You should eat something," Cassian said. "It's a long road ahead and you need your strength."

"Perhaps you're right."

She ignored the knots in her stomach as she picked up her spoon and dug in.

Chapter 11

Once their bellies were full—and Twill was quite drunk—Cassian tossed a few coins onto the table to pay for their meal. Twill staggered across the table, stumbling as she fought off a yawn. Ariadne had a hard time stopping the grin that erupted.

"You're drunk, little flame," she said on a laugh.

"Am not." But even as she said it, she tumbled to the table.

"Pick her up and let's go," Cassian said, agitated.

Ariadne scooped her up. The sylph curled into a ball in the palm of her hand and promptly fell asleep. Loud snores came from the small creature, which surprised Ariadne. She kept the hood pulled up, concealing her hair, and followed Cassian out of the tavern and into the ever-night.

The streets were less crowded. Folks appeared to be heading for their homes or the local inn. Ariadne stifled a yawn, the fatigue pounding through her.

"Can't we stay the night? I'm exhausted."

"We should keep moving," Cassian replied.

He took her by the elbow to lead her through the market square. But it was clear they weren't getting out of the town unnoticed. One of the vendors spoke to a man in a deep green cloak embroidered with glowing threads, its gold stitching pulsed faintly in the dark. The vendor pointed in their direction. The guard turned, his hand already on the curved hilt of his blade.

"Oh, no," she whispered.

"Yeah," Cassian agreed grimly.

Meanwhile, Twill continued to snore.

Cassian glanced over his shoulder, his body going taut. She followed his gaze. Two more guards had pushed into the crowd behind them. Their cloaks flared like banners of warning, and the sigil stitched across their chests blazed unnaturally bright.

The marketplace shifted in an instant. Vendors who'd been shouting prices moments ago now scrambled to close their stalls. Awnings collapsed, shutters slammed, silks and herbs yanked down with shaking hands. Spells flickered as magical wards sealed crates and cloaked booths in camouflage. No one wanted to be caught in the open.

Her pulse skipped.

"Who are they?" she asked, voice barely more than a breath.

Cassian didn't look at her. "The usurper's men. Look at their cloaks."

She did and froze.

A flaming star. Bold. Burning. Brazen.

It hit her like a blow to the chest. That sigil wasn't merely a symbol, it was a desecration. A corruption of starlight into something ravenous. The fire wasn't illumination. It was conquest. A twisted echo of everything she was supposed to be.

Her free hand curled into a fist.

It shouldn't hurt, but it did.

Cassian's grip tightened around her elbow as he veered down a side alley. She stumbled after him, heart pounding in her ears. There was nowhere to run. Doors were bolting shut one after another. Shops faded behind enchanted veils. Even the lanterns dimmed, their glow retreating like frightened eyes.

The inn they'd passed earlier was too far now. The road ahead narrowed. They were trapped. Rats in a gilded maze.

Behind them, cloaks flickered between shadows. Closer now.

And then, he appeared.

Eldrin the Wise stepped into the narrow lane as though drawn from the breath of the wind itself. His moss-colored robes flared as if catching unseen currents. Runes drifted across the hem like leaves stirred by a current of invisible power. He looked like a storm given shape. Ancient, deliberate, and dangerous in the way only time could be.

She and Cassian skidded to a halt.

The wizard didn't look at them. His silver eyes locked on the approaching guards. He raised one arm in a wide, deliberate arc. With the other, he thrust his hand forward—and the air split.

A ring of light bloomed midair, edged in fire that burned with a cold, unnatural gleam, like frost catching flame. Inside the circle shimmered a landscape not their own. Snow-covered ridges, endless night, and the jagged silhouette of a distant, claw-like peak.

"Quick as you can," Eldrin said, urgently, his voice like a bell struck deep within stone.

Cassian's voice was tight. "What are you doing here?"

Eldrin didn't flinch. "Saving the realm. Through the portal, dearies. No time to waste."

Ariadne's breath caught. The guards were almost upon them. She felt Twill curled against her palm, still fast asleep, utterly unaware.

Cassian turned to her, eyes asking the question he didn't voice.

Was she ready?

No. Absolutely not.

She nodded anyway.

With one hand, she clutched Twill to her chest. With the other, she grabbed Cassian's.

Together, they leapt into the ring of light.

Wind slammed into her on the other side, stealing her breath. The cold hit like a physical force, slicing across her skin sharp as star-forged steel. Her hood tore back. Her braid was nothing more than a loose plait now. Her glowing hair lit the night like a comet's tail as they plunged into a world cloaked in darkness and silence.

The wind howled through her cloak as her boots crunched on frostbitten grass, her hand still tangled with Cassian's. In her other, the sleeping Twill.

Ahead, the summit loomed. The Whitefire Tower stood tall against the night sky, its spire glowing softly, kissed by starlight. It was carved from stone so pale it nearly vanished against the landscape, the sky. Above it, a churning, swirling miasma of light. She stared at it with her heart in her throat trying to understand what she was seeing. In the center, a hot, dense core. Like a star about to shed its last light. Pulsing softly in the cradle of night. The edges rippled ever so slightly, as if space bent around it.

Deep in her bones, she sensed the low thrum with every pulse of light. The star sensed her presence and knew she returned home.

"The heart of Starna. The last star left in the original nine gates." His voice was low, and reverent.

Ariadne's breath misted in front of her, pluming white as she breathed out a shuddering breath of uncertainty. She didn't feel ready. But the stars were no longer waiting.

She clutched the pendant, the thread vibrating through the glass against her hand.

"It's time to go," he urged quietly.

She swallowed hard. Together, hand in hand, they began their trek.

A steep staircase was carved into the side of the summit winding upward. The climb was difficult, and she jostled Twill more than once. When the sylph awoke from her nap, she surged upward, twirling as a ball of light, momentarily disoriented.

"Where are we? What happened? This doesn't look like the village." She flew higher and higher and then dove back down to hover next to Ariadne's face. "That's the Elysian Summit."

"Yes, it is," she agreed with a nod, trying to remain calm. The closer they got to the summit, the more her nerves jangled.

"How did we get here?"

"The wizard sent us here," she replied.

"The wizard." Twill sank to Ariadne's shoulder, putting a hand to her head and groaning. "I missed out on a lot."

"You did," Cassian agreed. "And we're almost to the top."

Her gut was in a tight knot as they approached the top. Her legs burned with the exertion. She envied Twill who perched on her shoulder when she tired of flying. Her lungs ached from breathing heavy in the cold air. She was grateful for the cloak that kept her warm, even if it no longer served the purpose of covering her hair.

The braid had all but unraveled. It fluttered behind her, dragging the ground.

She did not know what would happen once they reached the top. It seemed far too easy for them to come this far and not encounter the usurper's men or the usurper himself. How could the three of them fight back? How could they complete the task at hand?

Beyond that, she wasn't even sure *what* the task at hand *was* other than opening the gate. How was she to do that? She had the Starshard, yes, and the pendant, but...her braid was another matter. The closer they got to the top, the brighter it beamed. Like a beacon in the night.

As the Celestial Gate churned with its furious light overhead, she started to understand her part in all of this. She and her braid were meant to come to this place.

Cassian was the first to arrive at the top of the summit. Ahead of him, the Whitefire Tower loomed bright and hot. He came to a shuddering halt. Ariadne had to tense to keep from running into the back of him. Twill, still on her shoulder, sucked in a quiet breath.

There, standing in front of them, were ten men. And in the center, one who looked as though he were carved from shadow and starlight. He didn't wear armor. He didn't have to. His pale hair was slicked back from his high forehead showing off his face that was far too beautiful to be human. He peered at her with dark, terrible eyes that felt as though they bored through to her soul.

This was a man who traded his soul, his life force, for the power that resided in the sky overhead. This was a man who ruled the realm of Starna with an iron fist. This was the man known only as the usurper.

"Starborn," he greeted with a terrible, cold voice. "You've returned at last. I've been waiting for you. Welcome home."

Cassian planted himself between the two of them as though a human shield, one hand on the hilt of his sword, the other hovering over the bronze medallion resting on his chest. Twill hissed in her ear.

"That's the one the tree's whisper about."

Ariadne's heart thundered in her chest. Terror rose through her. This was the one who stole her throne, her realm. And she was the one the gods created to defeat him.

It seemed a wholly impossible task.

"Though I doubt this is the homecoming you dreamed of, is it?" he continued. His mouth curled into a smile that didn't reach his eyes. "I cannot allow you to come one more step."

"You cannot change destiny," Cassian said, his voice loud and strong and sure. "She is here. And you will be defeated."

He laughed a mirthless laugh. One that cut right through her, making her bones vibrate. As though he chewed on starlight and spit it back out.

"You are a traitor, guardian. And you will be dealt with."

Twill launched her tiny body into the sky and headed for them as if she intended to attack. Ariadne sucked in a sharp breath.

The usurper smacked her down as though she were nothing more than a pesky mosquito. The little sylph crashed to the stone ground, her light fading and her wings coming to a terrible halt.

"Twill!"

Ariadne started to take a step toward her small friend when Cassian put up a hand to stop her.

"Cage the little menace," the usurper said with a sneer. "Bring me the girl. I want her hair. Then toss the traitorous guardian in the dungeon where he can rot out the rest of his betraying days."

Ariadne's stomach dropped as the soldiers advanced, boots crunching on frost, metal glinting beneath their cloaks. She felt Cassian shift beside her. He cast her a quick glance over his shoulder.

She couldn't read his expression, but she didn't need to.

This was it. They'd come all this way. Fought. Bled. Believed. And now they were going to lose.

Twill let out a furious screech and shot into the air, but the soldiers were fast, enchanted nets in hand, magic swirling at their fingertips.

Ariadne's heart slammed against her ribs. She refused to fail.

Not like this. Not before she reached the Gate. Not before she chose who she was meant to be. Not before she tried.

Before the men reached her, her braid flamed to life. Brilliant. Bright. Blazing.

They would not be captured. They would not be rotting in a dungeon. And they would not be defeated.

The Starshard in her pocket soared to life the same moment her braid flared. She brought it out, holding it up to the sky. Light seeped from her closed fingers. The men stumbled backward away from her, their faces contorted in shock.

From her net, Twill snarled, "Let me go. You can't keep me caged like I'm an animal."

As she said it, the ring on her forefinger came to life, glowing and pulsing much like Ariadne's hair. The net shuddered around her. She stopped struggling against her bonds. The moment she did, the net disintegrated around her, falling to the ground in a heap of cords. With her ring still showing signs of life, she launched upward into the sky as nothing more than pulsing golden light.

She dive-bombed the soldiers with an ear-piercing war cry.

"That thing is a pest. Get her under control!" the usurper ordered.

"That *thing* is my friend," Ariadne said.

Without thinking, she swung the Starshard in a wide arc. The light bouncing off it connected with the man holding Cassian. The guard cried out when the light seared through him, releasing Cassian. He ducked in the nick of time, getting out of the line of fire.

Meanwhile, Twill kept the others busy as she continued to dive bomb them like a crazed bird protecting her young.

"Get to the tower," Cassian ordered. "Hurry!" He unsheathed his sword and charged toward the other guards.

Her heart was in her throat. "But—"

"Go, Ari!"

Using the Starshard to carve a path for her, she bolted into a run toward the tower. Behind her the usurper shouted a curse. Something slammed into the center of her back, sending her sprawling. The Starshard tumbled from her hand, clattering on the ground before her. She scrambled to her feet, her eye fixed on the piece of fallen star ahead.

But as she did, someone snatched her by the braid and gave her a jerk backward. She fell back, landing hard on the ground to peer up into the terrifying eyes of the usurper. He raised the dagger in his hand, the light from the overhead churning gate winking off the steel.

He was going to cut her hair.

Oh, gods, no.

She fumbled with the dagger at her waist. But her trembling fingers were unable to grasp it. A shriek from somewhere behind the usurper. In a violent jerk, he released her. Ariadne rolled to her side and got to her hands and knees in time to see Twill attacking his head.

Wasting no time, she scrambled for the Starshard, snatching it up and leaping to her feet. She bolted into a run, pushing her legs to go faster and faster. Her muscles burned from the exertion. Her breath see-sawed in and out of her, the cold air scorching her lungs.

The High Queen said to climb the highest tower. It was within her sights. She cast a glance over her shoulder to see Cassian handling the usurper's men and Twill handling the usurper. He swatted at her as though she were an annoying gnat, which kept him busy.

He didn't see when Ariadne entered the tower.

With her hand on the wall, she started up the curved staircase that went up and up and up. Every muscle in her body was on fire. Every breath she sucked in and out was more difficult than the last. Every thought was only that of getting to the top of the tower.

She'd decide what to do once she got to the top.

The moment she stepped off the last step and onto the landing, something ancient stirred in the howling wind. The words of the prophecy wrapped around her. Whispered in the gusts as though it recognized her. As though it knew her. The summit, the stars, the gate above. All of it.

Born of blood under a ruined sky.

Bound by an unbreakable oath, a binding pact to mend a fractured world.

When the stars fall, and the strand breaks, the gate shall open.

Above her, the center of the maelstrom of light flickered. The sky churned. The clouds stirred. And in the center of it all, the light of the star. Glimmering. Flickering. Glowing.

"*When the strand breaks, the gate shall open,*" she whispered.

Glancing down, she saw the silver thread in the pendant reacting with its own pulsing glow. The wizard's words came back to her, too.

The stars whisper, but they do not command. You are not the braid, child. You are the loom. When the world insists there is only one way forward, let this remind you that your light was born to choose another.

She'd run toward her destiny. From the first moment Cassian told her about the prophecy, that she was meant to return to Starna, that she was prophesied to reclaim her birthright, she was terrified. Now, that fear vanished. The light inside her ignited, burning bright and hot like the star above her head.

The pendant hanging around her neck warmed, the light matching that of the glimmering, flowing, flickering star. Her hair gleamed.

Shouts below. Cassian's voice urging her to hurry.

She pulled her braid over her shoulder, the plait unraveling and loose.

"This does not define me," she whispered. "This remakes me."

She pressed the pendant against her hair, tucking it between one of the loose plaits.

"Let this be the light that breaks through the darkness," she said.

The silver strands flared with celestial light. Moonlight and starlight merging into one luminous amalgamation. The cord around her neck snapped and disintegrated. That left her holding the Starshard.

She held it by the narrow end, then ran her finger across the edge. It felt sharp enough.

As her hair blazed bright, she lifted the edge of the Starshard to the nape of her neck, holding her hair in the fist of her other hand. And then with a swift stroke, she cut through the strands. Then another and another until finally, the braid was fully severed.

The glass pendant shattered, the pieces landing at her feet. The spiral coil that was once part of the pendant unraveled, swirling around the thick braid as though tightening its grip around the thick plait.

Divine starlight.

On impulse, she tossed her hair upward along with the Starshard toward the white dwarf star. It accepted it as though it was an offering to the gods.

The moment the braid left her hand, something inside her tore loose. A flash of light, then a white-hot flame burst in her chest.

Her hair unraveled midair, threads of silver disintegrated into starlight. A flash of light. And then a bright white flame. Her magic surged, a violent rush tearing through her spine, down her limbs. Too much. Too fast. Not like fire. Like truth.

The Gate awakened.

Threads of glowing silver unfurled throughout the sky like spun silk pulled taut across the heavens. Constellations were unmade and remade. The tower beneath her feet pulsed, rumbled, vibrated with ancient power. The wind screamed. The swirling clouds spun faster and faster around the expanding star until there were no more clouds and then, suddenly, a resounding crack split the sky like bone breaking.

The force knocked her off her feet. She hit the stone ground hard, the breath knocked from her lungs. Light rushed through her blood, her breath, her bones. Her back arched. Her fingers clawed the ground.

She wasn't just severed from the braid. She was unbound. The magic that lived dormant inside her awoke and unfurled its wings, stretching its expanse through her entire being.

Above her, the gate split wide. The sky fractured. Light scattered like lightning made of stars. The realm above took a deep, cleansing breath, sucking up all the light. Gathering it together. And then a brilliant flash, roaring with radiance.

The clouds disappeared. Bursting across the darkened sky, a comet pushed its way across it trailing stardust in its wake. Leaving behind the brilliant indigo sky. Light rippled in glorious waves. The stars above flared brighter than any she'd ever seen.

And then—stillness. The kind that comes at the dawning of a new age.

The usurper's magic was broken. Starna was free.

And so was she.

CHAPTER 12

Ariadne remained on the ground, staring up at the strange sky. At stars she did not recognize. The cold seeped into her skin, deeper than it should have, as if the night air could reach her soul now. But she didn't mind.

The howling wind had calmed.

Even the shouts from below had gone quiet.

The silence around her wasn't peaceful. It was piercing. Hollow. The world had broken and wove itself back together.

She sat up slowly, her body sluggish and unsteady, as though something vital had been torn from her.

Something vital *had* been torn from her. It streaked across the ever-night sky.

Tentatively, she reached for her head. Her fingers brushed the jagged ends of her hair—cut uneven. Her braid...gone. The weight of it, the anchor of her whole life, had vanished. The absence was almost nauseating.

A tremor moved through her.

Her vision blurred for half a heartbeat, the sky spinning above her like a wheel of starlight and shadow. A pulse of ancient magic thudded through her chest, then faded.

And still, the sky burned.

Her gaze fixed on the comet blazing across the heavens. It shimmered silver-gold, trailing stardust like a promise. Like a memory. Like a braid.

As it pushed forward, it cleaved the dark clouds in its wake, scattering them like ash. The unfamiliar constellations emerged behind it—dazzling, bright, utterly new.

Ariadne placed a hand over her heart.

She changed. She *awakened.*

And yet, she smiled.

A ball of glowing fire was suddenly in her line of vision.

"You did it, Starborn! Best quest ever!"

She held out her hand for Twill. The sylph landed in her palm, light as a feather. Her wings, however, continued to flutter behind her in a brilliant iridescent blur. Her face creased with a broad smile as she gazed up with her golden eyes.

"You freed us."

"With your help," she replied with a grin.

Twill held up her hand showing off the ring the wizard gave her. The magic inside it continued to pulse.

"With the help of the Unbinding Ring." She turned her hand to and fro, admiring it. "It's like he knew."

"Perhaps he did," Ariadne agreed, thinking of the pendant that was now part of the comet streaking across the sky.

She wondered about Cassian's medallion. Had he, too, used it?

Twill's gaze lifted to the sky, as if she noticed the comet for the first time. "That looks like your braid, Starborn."

"It is," she said, her words soft.

The burden of her long hair was no more. Now, it was part of this world.

Footsteps behind her made her turn. Cassian stumbled onto the landing from the stairs. One hand gripped the cord of the medallion around his neck. In his other, his blood-stained sword. From across the way, their eyes met. Her heart leapt to see him standing there. Blood stained the front of his tunic. Dirt smudged his face. He looked as though he'd been to hell and back. And perhaps he had.

"Stardust."

She climbed to her feet. He dropped his sword. Twill twirled into the air.

Cassian and Ariadne came together, falling into each other's arms. His hand immediately went to her hair, his fingers tangling in the short lengths. He tilted her head back. She looked up into his vibrant blue eyes.

There was such admiration and adoration there she nearly came undone.

"I never doubted you," he said.

Then his lips captured hers, stealing her breath and making her heart swell. When she thought her world could not tilt anymore, it did. His arms tightened around her as though she belonged there with him, pulling her close. The world blurred around them and for a moment, there was nothing else. No crumbling tower. No shattered sky. No prophecy burning in her blood.

For one suspended moment, there was no starlight in her veins. No gods whispering fate. No guardian sworn to protect her.

Just a girl who had waited her whole life for this feeling. Just a man who kissed her like she was made of something sacred. And under the watchful hush of the stars, they weren't legends or destinies. They were only themselves.

And it was enough.

When he pulled back, he gazed at her in wonder as though she was something rare and miraculous. His voice was hushed with wonder. "Your hair…"

"It's in the sky," Twill said, excitement edging her voice. She hovered over the two of them, her glow brighter than usual.

But he never took his gaze off her.

"I know," he murmured, giving her a soft smile. His thumb brushed over the curve of her cheekbone. It sent tendrils of warmth spiraling through her.

He studied her with a tenderness she hadn't seen before. "It doesn't glow anymore. Not like it did before."

"No?"

He shook his head as he wrapped a short strand around his forefinger. "It's the color of spun silk. Pale as stardust."

Her heart fluttered. The light might be gone from her hair, but it was clear that, in his eyes, she still shone just as brightly.

"The usurper?" she asked.

"The moment the spell broke, so did he," Cassian replied. He pressed his forehead against hers, as though he didn't want to elaborate.

She didn't understand what that meant. Perhaps she didn't want to know what had happened to the usurper. She assumed he was dead.

He took her by the hand. Together, they walked to the wall where they looked out onto the mountains surrounding the Whitefire Tower. Before the spell broke, the land was covered in a shadowy darkness. Now, moonlight and starlight beamed down in a soft blue-white illumination showcasing the jagged peaks of the snow-capped mountains.

"It has been many years since moonlight touched our land." He nodded toward the sky.

She followed his gaze. Two crescent moons burned bright white, nestled against each other surrounded by twinkling stars. In the distance, the comet continued burning its path.

"This is where you were born. Did you know that?"

She shook her head.

"And this," he pointed upward, "is the Celestial Gate they secreted you through."

She looked up but saw nothing but clear sky and twinkling lights. "I don't see anything."

Cassian moved to stand behind her, wrapping his arms around her and holding her. "Keep looking," he whispered in her ear.

As she peered at the sky above, she saw the flicker then. Almost imperceptible as the light fluttered through a circular gate. And in the center, where the dwarf star had been, there was the hint of a warm glow. The hint of the Starshard that now resided there.

"Only a Guardian can open it now."

She lowered her gaze and looked down at his clasped hands around her. She snuggled closer to him, seeking his warmth in the chill that swept off the summit. "Like you. Will you go back now? To the Temple of Silence?"

The question hung between them. He didn't answer. His body stilled against hers. She shivered, waiting for his response. Hoping and fearing at the same time.

Finally, he said, "You are ruler now. It is your choice."

She turned in the circle of his arms and looked up at him. Moonlight carved silver across the planes of his face. Her gaze landed on the medallion still hanging around his neck. She traced the star-spun spiral with the tip of her finger.

"I don't feel like a ruler. The wizard said to speak your truth into it. I cannot walk through this realm without you at my side."

"Is that your truth?" he asked.

"It is."

His hand closed over hers where it still touched the medallion. "Then I speak mine. I choose you over my duty as Guardian of Knowledge."

The spiral glowed.

A sudden warmth pulsed between their hands as the medallion lit from within. They broke apart, startled, as the spiral unspooled from its setting, lifting into the air like a delicate ribbon of starlight suspended between them.

A voice, ancient and resonant, wove itself into the wind.

"Your vow to the Temple of Silence has been released, Guardian," said the Goddess of Echoes.

When the words drifted away, so, too, did the light hovering between them. Her breath pooled in her throat. He was free. Not because he abandoned his duty, but because he fulfilled it. Because he chose her.

Twill appeared between them, bright and bouncing in the air. "Don't mind me! I'm over here pretending I didn't sob through that entire magical declaration of love." She punctuated that with a dramatic sniff.

Which made Ariadne and Cassian both laugh.

"And, Starborn, now that you're Celestial Queen and all, don't forget about us little folks, eh?"

"How could I?" Ariadne said with a laugh, her heart light.

"Good!" Twill did a delighted somersault in midair. "Because I'm claiming the guest room in the royal treehouse."

Then she fluttered up and away, leaving behind a trail of shimmering gold dust.

Cassian stepped beside Ariadne and took her hand, anchoring her with his touch. "Come on, stardust. Let's go home."

She squeezed his fingers, lifted her chin, and together they turned toward the waiting horizon.

And for the first time, the stars did not watch her. They followed.

Also by Michelle Miles

Age of Wizards (Epic Fantasy)

In the Tower of the Wizard King

On the Hunt for the Wizard King

Dragon Protectors (Paranormal Shifter Romance)

Desiring the Dragon Lord

Seducing the Dragon Knight

Tempting Her Dragon Bodyguard

Dragon Protectors Book Collection, Books 1-3

Dream Walker (Urban Fantasy)

Call of the Dark

Blood and Bone

Flame and Fury

Smoke and Ashes

Light of the World

Dream Walker Collection (Books 1-5)

Divin Heir: Dream Walker Origins

Enchanted Realms (YA Fantasy Romance)

Once Upon an Ancient Curse (Red Riding Hood)

Once Upon a Silver Strand (Rapunzel)

Once Upon a Midnight Clear (Cinderella)

Once Upon True Love's Kiss (Snow White)

Once Upon an Enchanted Kiss (Sleeping Beauty)

Once Upon an Enchanted Castle (Beauty & the Beast)

Five Towers (YA Fantasy)

The Sorcerer's Daughter

**Highland Destiny (Paranormal Romance)
Coming Fall 2025**

Desiring the Highland Laird

Loving the Highland Warrior

Captivating the Highland Rogue

**Ransom & Fortune Adventures
(Time Travel Action/Adventure)**

Highland Fling, Vol 1

Dead of Winter, Vol 2

The Citadel, Vol 3

Lord of the Underworld, Vol 4

Realm of Honor (Fantasy Romance)

One Knight Only

Only for a Knight

A Knight to Remember

A Knight Like No Other

Shadows of the Knight

Realm of Honor Collection (Books 1-5)

Shorts and Anthologies (Fantasy/Paranormal)

Newsletter Subscribers Only

A Dance Among the Faeries, A Short Story

Eorwulf, A Short Story

Dragons of Emhain, Short Story Collection

Watch for more at www.MichelleMiles.net

About the Author

MICHELLE MILES believes in fairy tales, true love, and a little bit of magic in every story. She writes fantasy, paranormal, and young adult books packed with adventure, action, and swoon-worthy romance—because what's a story without a bit of danger and a whole lot of heart? From angels and demons to dragons, elves, and time travelers, her books are filled with epic quests, fierce heroines, and the kind of heroes worth falling for.

When she's not crafting new adventures, she brings stories to life as a narrator and hosts *Miles Beyond the Page*, a podcast where she chats with authors about their writing journeys. A Texas girl through and through, she loves getting lost in a good book, binge-watching movies, hiking the trails, and sipping a glass of wine. Come hang out with her on Facebook, Instagram, Pinterest, and more!

Magical Worlds, Daring Adventures, Unforgettable Romance!

Read more at MichelleMiles.net